The Truth Seekers Mystery Series

Dinosaur Quest
at Diamond Peak

By

Christina and Felice Gerwitz

The Truth Seekers: Those dedicated to finding the truth...

John: 8:32

"Jesus then said... ...and you will know the truth and the truth will make you free."

This book is dedicated to Neal William Gerwitz

The Truth Seekers Mystery Series:

1. *The Missing Link: Found*

2. *Dinosaur Quest at Diamond Peak*

The Truth Seekers Mystery Series

Dinosaur Quest
at Diamond Peak

By

Christina and Felice Gerwitz

Media Angels®
Fort Myers, Florida

Dinosaur Quest at Diamond Peak
Copyright © 2001 by Christina N. Gerwitz and Felice Gerwitz
ISBN # 0-9700385-6-9

Published by Media Angels ®
Ft. Myers, Florida 33912

Scripture verses from The Holy Bible RSV
Ignatius Press San Francisco Copyright © 1966.

All of the events pertaining to the characters and the characters in this
book are fictitious.

Cover Illustration by Home Based Publishing

Printed in the United States of America

Table of Contents

Chapter 1
Gone Wrong

Christian adjusted the chinstrap on his blue helmet and checked his sky diving equipment yet again. From this distance, the three-story buildings resembled toy models. Christian swallowed in nervous anticipation while the Twin Otter bounced through turbulence on its way to its cruising altitude at 10,000 feet. He glanced at the white-haired pilot and also the three other occupants seated on metal benches at the rear of the plane.

Petite, fifteen-year-old Anna Murphy sat beside her tall, muscular older brother Christian and across from Phil Rogers and his ten-year-old daughter Carolyn. Anna brushed her short, light-brown hair away from her eyes, and steadied herself as she focused her 35 mm camera. She captured pictures of Phil, who was wearing a blue and green striped jumpsuit, deep in conversation with his daughter Carolyn. She snapped another shot of Christian, this time studying the aerial photograph of the drop zone as he readied himself to dive.

Anna grinned for the hundredth time and then chided

herself because she could hardly quit smiling long enough to take another picture. She was in the air with Phil Rogers, a world-renown skydiver! A Christian magazine, *God's Truth*, had hired her father, Dr. Jack Murphy, to photograph Phil in action for an upcoming issue. Phil was known to use his talents as a springboard for sharing his faith with others.

"Do you think Dad is at the drop zone yet?" Anna shouted to be heard over the loud engine.

"Probably," Christian agreed nodding his head, knowing his father waited at the airstrip below.

Just as his children had suspected, their father had already set up the sophisticated photographic equipment waiting for the spellbinding sight of Phil's next jump. Dr. Murphy stood tall and lean, his blond hair showing signs of gray, as it gleamed in the sunlight. He shaded his eyes and squinted up, as he watched the plane gain altitude. He would soon need to use binoculars.

Behind him the open field of rolling grass stirred in the gentle breeze. A large area close to the tarmac had been maintained as the skydiving drop zone. This would be the place where Phil and Christian would land. Phil was known for his unique jump style. Jack was an avid skydiver as was his son Christian; yet, he had never participated in skydiving competitions. He knew that well-seasoned skydivers, like Phil, were known to do trick maneuvers with their sport parachutes. Using a pull or control knob allowed the skydiver to regulate the direction of escaping air giving him more maneuverability while airborne. Phil was also able to perform a number of stunts during his free-fall, such as a backward rapid spin. Jack was hoping to photograph this phenomenal feat.

Jack switched his attention to the sky, now squinting through a pair of high-powered binoculars. The Twin Otter plane, affectionately named Clara, just sliced through the clouds. Quincy leveled the plane out at 13,500 feet, the optimum altitude for skydiving.

Phil Rogers stood grasping the handles mounted to both sides of the plane's open rear door. Although Phil had made thousands of jumps, he was anxious to be off.

8

"One more picture!" Anna shouted to be heard.

Phil, attired in a jumpsuit, goggles, helmet, gloves, and a sport parachute, turned slightly to grin over his shoulder at the camera.

Carolyn smiled at her father and shouted her customary, "Godspeed, Dad!" It had been her parting shot for as long as she could remember. She often accompanied her father on his sky dives and always yelled these precious words right before her father leaped from a plane. The comment was their own private joke, for he would be traveling at speeds of up to 200 mph.

Phil acknowledged Carolyn with a smile and thumbs up; he then turned his attention back to the open door, getting ready. In seconds the plane would approach the drop zone, and it would be time to jump. Phil mentally did a countdown, five ... four ... three ... two ... one ... and then flung himself into the air.

The plane suddenly felt empty to Carolyn without her father and she rose to sit next to Anna. "Someday I'll be old enough to jump," Carolyn said. "But right now I'm scared."

Anna was surprised by the revelation. For some reason, Anna also had a feeling of apprehension. However, she smiled to reassure the younger girl.

Christian stood and took Phil's spot at the open door. He would jump exactly two minutes behind Phil. In addition to his jumpsuit, goggles, and helmet Christian wore an altimeter and regulation parachute. Staring down into Florida's open grasslands, Christian watched as Phil performed several stunts before effortlessly sailing earthward. Just as he was about to jump, Christian felt the plane tip and pick up speed.

What is Quincy doing? He passed the drop zone! Christian thought as his hands automatically tightened on the handles. His worry turned to astonishment as he turned and saw Quincy making his way to the rear of the plane, leaving the cockpit unattended.

"Quincy!" Christian yelled. The roar of the wind rushed through his helmet as Christian tried to withstand the buffeting force of the rushing air. Before Christian could utter another word, the plane suddenly hit an air pocket and tipped again. This time the force was too great and Christian fell out into the empty sky.

Snatched from the plane, Christian caught only the last of a sharp scream. He glanced back just in time to see Carolyn sliding toward the open door.

"No-o-o!" Christian shouted as he closed his eyes, refusing to acknowledge what he was about to see.

"Anna!" Carolyn screamed in terror as the young girl slid closer to the open door.

Without thinking, Anna instinctively, threw herself onto the floor hooking her own foot around the bench leg, and grabbed Carolyn's shirt just in time. Anna pulled with all her might and slowly eased the girl away from danger. The plane righted itself, giving Carolyn the benefit of gravity. Anna continued to pull. The young girl was almost away from the open door. Anna sighed in relief, thinking the crisis had passed. She would soon find out she was wrong, dead wrong.

Suddenly Anna yelled in agony and could no longer hold onto Carolyn, who slid through the open door and out of the plane.

Chapter 2
Drop Zone

Christian normally loved skydiving, but not today. He was too worried about Anna, Carolyn, and the pilot. *Why did Quincy leave his post? Would they make it down safely?* Christian could only wonder and pray.

Christian fell belly first, his arms and legs spread wide. He mentally went over the landing drill. A skydiver's landing pattern was similar to that of a plane and began with a downwind approach past the drop zone. He would then execute a ninety-degree turn in toward the target, fly parallel with the drop zone, and perform a final upwind approach. This would allow him to descend, brake, and glide into the landing area.

The ground was still so far away that it didn't seem to get any nearer. *What if the parachute doesn't open?* Christian shook his head, denying himself the indulgence of fear. Instead, he concentrated on the drop zone far below. He could see the green grassy field alongside the tarmac, and what he knew from experience was the drop zone close behind. He saw that Phil was just reaching the ground. From this angle, Christian could already tell that he would not be able to make the landing near Phil.

About sixty seconds later, at 4,500 feet, Christian pulled the ripcord, waiting in anticipation for the few seconds that it would take to deploy the rectangular shaped parachute.

Whoosh! The ram-air parachute opened wide as the shoulder straps hauled Christian up. He soon slowed to a mere 10 mph. As soon as he dropped to the ground he'd figure out a way to help Anna and Carolyn. He dreaded telling his Dad and Phil what had happened.

I wonder if I can still see the Twin Otter? Christian thought momentarily looking back. If it was possible for Christian's heart to stop beating due to sheer panic, no doubt it would happen now. As he focused in on the plane, his blood seemed to run cold. All that could be seen was a dark silhouette against the clear sky. He instantly recognized it was Carolyn! She tumbled toward Christian, rapidly gaining on him in a free-fall as he was drifting along more slowly.

Christian closed his eyes, willing the sight to disappear. He immediately opened them, and he could see Carolyn's mouth opening and closing in panic. It seemed like only a second before she rocketed past him, arms, and legs flailing, on her way toward oblivion.

Christian yelled in frustrated anger. He began to pray for God's help and mercy. A welcoming sense of peace assured him that God was in control. He set his jaw in determination completely focused on the mission. Only with Divine help could Carolyn be saved from certain death. He couldn't allow Phil to watch his only daughter fall to her death when he could possibly prevent it. Christian needed to attempt a risky move, which he had only read about in books, in order to save Carolyn. He had never done a cutaway! Uttering another quick prayer heavenward, Christian got into position. Christian knew if the parachute detachment was not done properly that he could lose all control. It was one of a sky divers worse nightmares.

He flattened his body and reached under his right chest strap for the soft handle held in place by Velcro. He pulled on the cutaway handle. A split-second later, his parachute jettisoned, and Christian was once again free-falling toward the ground. With his hands extended over his head, Christian aimed straight down. This aerodynamic position allowed Christian to gain on Carolyn, as she continued to tumble, her arms and legs still flailing. He was able to cut the air drag and reached a speed of almost 250 mph.

Help me Lord! He prayed as the distance shortened, he headed straight for Carolyn.

Did he have enough time? Christian ducked his head as he slashed through the wind; his goggles were pulled taut across his face from the extreme wind pressure. Christian continued his downward dive. Seconds seemed to pass like hours, and then he was a mere 50 feet from Carolyn. Christian glanced at his altimeter refusing to think about what would happen if he did not reach her in time.

As he neared Carolyn, Christian wanted to throw himself at her, but couldn't just yet. His timing had to be perfect, but to make matters worse she was still tumbling.

Another precious second passed before Christian flattened himself. Now they were both falling at about the same speed. He reached his hand out, and made a desperate grab for her.

Contact!

Carolyn screamed but all Christian could see was her open mouth. It was useless to talk while in a free-fall.

I've made it! I'm here! Christian joyously thought. As if in slow motion, Christian pulled until he was able to grab Carolyn from behind, around her waist. Twice he almost lost his hold on her, but miraculously they remained together. Carolyn latched onto Christian's arms with a death grip.

Christian briefly took his eyes off Carolyn, to see the ground seeming to rise up to swallow them. Without further hesitation, he removed his left hand from her hold and yanked on the reserve handle to activate his backup parachute. He immediately replaced his arm around her waist, as her nails again dug into his arm.

As Christian waited those timeless seconds, he reminded

himself that their fate was in God's hands. Carolyn was held securely by Christian as the seconds ticked for *when*, he stubbornly thought, not *if* the backup parachute opened.

The spring loaded pilot chute suddenly snapped open, deploying the reserve parachute and snatching them up. Christian hooted. "Yes!" He smiled broadly as Carolyn joined his whoop with one of her own only seconds before she began to cry in relief.

The tiny figures of his Dad and Phil below, gave Christian hope that help would be waiting when they landed. He prayed they would succeed despite the odds. It made little difference that they were only 2500 feet off the ground. *The parachute will slow us down, won't it?* Christian ignored the question for thinking about it was futile, and he forced it out of his head. Christian wished he had more experience, but felt he had done everything that was humanly possible.

Leaning close to Carolyn's ear, he yelled, "Do what I do!"

Carolyn simply nodded, too shaken to reply.

Christian straightened and pulled Carolyn back as they both pointed their feet toward the onrushing ground. The landing would be tricky. They had not only missed the drop zone, but also the entire airstrip by hundreds of feet. They would be landing somewhere in the grassy field beyond the airstrip. Who knew what was hidden in the tall grass — perhaps some piece of rusting machinery. It was impossible for Christian to maneuver the parachute, or brake, because he had Carolyn in his arms. So this left them with little choice, but to land were the wind took them. He knew better than to try to make a radical turn on the final approach, which might cause them to lose altitude even faster.

A short time later, they plummeted into the tall grass. Christian instinctively forced Carolyn to the left while he rolled in the opposite direction. Waves of relief rushed over Christian upon impact, as the wind was momentarily knocked out of him.

Christian slowly rose to his feet, checking to see that he could stand, ignoring the tangled up parachute, and everything else for that matter. He was just glad to be alive! Unlatching his parachute, he stiffly half-trotted, half-walked over to Carolyn who lay only a few feet away. Carolyn didn't move. She was lying on her side. Christian watched as her whole body shook. She was crying. She was alive!

Christian awkwardly looked away wondering what to do now. Relief flooded him as he saw both their dads racing toward him through the high grass.

Turning back to Carolyn he said, "It's going to be all right."

Fifty feet away, Dr. Murphy breathlessly yelled, "Are you guys okay?"

Christian nodded and then motioned to Carolyn. "I'm fine, but I don't know about her," he yelled back.

Phil sprinted past Dr. Murphy in his haste to reach his daughter's side. Gingerly he searched for injuries, and then finding none he pulled her close into his arms and began praising God. Dr. Murphy, close behind, made his way over to the three. Almost there, he shouted and waved, "Great job Christian! I'm so proud ..." Suddenly his words were cut off as he sank to the ground with a grunt of pain.

Both Christian and Phil glanced back to see Dr. Murphy hunched over on the ground. His face was twisted in pain.

* * * * * * * *

An hour later Phil, Christian and an exhausted Carolyn sat in a small lunchroom at the local flight school. The three occupants were gathered together at one table near the back corner of the deserted room.

Although a paramedic had evaluated her on the scene, Carolyn was still in mild shock and not ready to talk. Carolyn leaned against her father contentedly as Phil and Christian spoke in hushed tones. Phil had already hugged Christian, patted him on the back, and shook his hand several times, telling him how thankful he was for saving his daughter's life. Embarrassed, Christian shifted their focus by acknowledging credit was due to Divine intervention as well as the author of his skydiving book, none other than Phil. He had indeed learned from the best. A few

15

months ago, Christian received a special exemption and obtained his skydiving certification at the age of 16, two years earlier than the law normally allowed.

They were waiting for Anna and Dr. Murphy to join them. The plane had landed, but they still were uncertain as to what had transpired after Christian's descent.

"Are you okay?" Christian asked jumping up to help as his dad and Anna walked in. He stared at Anna; she looked a bit ruffled yet thankfully she was alive. Their dad, however, came in limping, and leaning on Anna for support. His badly sprained, left ankle, was turning shades of purple and blue, and was already swollen to twice its normal size. The paramedics had urged Dr. Murphy to seek immediate attention, and he assured them that he would have his ankle x-rayed.

They all asked Dr. Murphy about his ankle. "I'm fine," he replied, sheepishly explaining that he had stepped into a hole.

Joining the others around the table, Anna began to tell how Carolyn had fallen out of the airplane and her own harrowing experience.

At first Anna shrugged helplessly, not sure where to begin. She finally went into a brief description of how the plane had lurched, hitting an air pocket, and how she had tried to pull Carolyn away from the open door. "Quincy had left the cockpit and was just standing there. When the plane jerked again, he saw that I needed help. The poor man was trying to grab a hold of Carolyn, but in the process he stepped on me! I lost my grip, and then Quincy fell down on top of me and accidentally rolled into Carolyn. This sent Carolyn out of the plane with Quincy almost following." Anna paused, her eyes were sparkling with unshed tears as she slowly relived the incident. "It was horrible!" she finally said, shuddering.

Phil nodded as he patiently waited for Anna to continue.

Anna held her emotions in check and gathered her thoughts. "I jumped up and started to yell at Quincy; but, after I took one look at his face I could see something was wrong." Anna shook her head, "I didn't know what to do. He looked disoriented. One side of his face was droopy, and he went to sit on the bench. A voice seemed to say, 'Get him to the cockpit,' and I numbly obeyed, while wondering where it came from. I said, 'You have got to land this plane.' I didn't know what had happened to him. I finally convinced Quincy that we needed to land the plane. He followed me as if he were in a daze. As soon as I got him back into the pilot's chair and strapped in, I realized that had it not been for autopilot, we would have certainly crashed."

Anna stopped and for the first time smiled, "It was amazing! As soon as I started praying, Quincy snapped out of it. His speech was a bit slurred, but he mentioned that you," Anna gestured toward Phil, "had a good jump. He didn't even mention Christian and Carolyn and I thought it better that I didn't either."

Anna's voice held all captive as she finished with, "I still don't understand it, but we just flew back as smooth as ever and Quincy brought the plane back here and made a perfect landing. It was the strangest thing. As soon as we got out of the plane, he started to act disoriented again and his slurred speech became worse."

Sitting back, she gave them time to digest the story.

Dr. Murphy was the first to break the silence, "Quincy has been taken to the hospital and is having some tests run. The paramedics suspected he may have suffered a mild stroke, but couldn't say for sure."

The five people fell silent as they each reflected on the days' events. Anna and Christian's heroic rescues were events they would always remember. The life-threatening circumstances that seemed to spell doom for each person could only be explained with one word—*miracle!*

Chapter 3
On Their Own

This time, at an elevation of 25,000 feet, Christian and Anna Murphy were traveling in a commercial aircraft. After their previous airplane escapade only several weeks earlier, both were excited but still a bit uneasy. At least the doors were firmly shut and Quincy was far away. He had suffered a stroke, but was on his way to recovery, vowing that he would eventually fly again.

The Murphys looked forward to a new adventure in Colorado. They planned to photograph an astounding paleontological discovery. Little did they suspect that they were about to embark on a quest that would shake the foundations of their faith, testing what they believed was the truth.

Christian shifted in his seat for the tenth time since leaving Fort Myers an hour earlier. Try as he might, no position seemed comfortable in the cramped middle seat. Looking away from his laptop computer screen, Christian rubbed his eye as he glanced over at his sister. "I still can't believe Dad let us come on our own."

"I wish his ankle had healed so that he could have come with us." Anna agreed.

Seeing the pensive expression on her face, Christian tried to lighten the mood. "Too bad there is nothing to be excited about." "Not excited?" she asked beginning to smile. "We're only on a two-week long vacation to a ski resort in Colorado." Christian grinned back, but Anna didn't give him a chance to reply as she continued. "This trip is absolutely no reason to be overjoyed! We are only going to be staying with philanthropists in their brand new, state-of-the-art home."

Christian held up his hands in mocking defeat. "Okay, I'll confess I'm happy to be going too, but not just about the vacation part."

Anna's brown eyes sparkled as she held up a picturesque postcard she was using as a bookmark. The snow-capped peaks and the array of colored trees showed a magnificent scene of Rocky Mountain National Park. "I can't wait to take pictures of the breathtaking scenery and," as Anna paused for emphasis, "of the fossilized dinosaur."

Christian's eyes warmed at the words. He was interested in becoming an archaeologist and, although paleontology was quite different, anything in the area of ancient studies interested him.

"And, I'm looking forward to meeting Grandma's and Grandpa's friends, Mr. and Mrs. Sullivan," Anna finished.

"I can't wait to see *them* either . . . the Sullivans I mean, not the dinosaur bones."

"Right, Christian," Anna laughed. "I know why you're really excited about our chance to come."

"Hey, give me a break. It's not every day I get to see the excavation of a dinosaur fossil."

"Aren't you glad it's a *Tyrannosaurus rex*?" Anna asked.

"It doesn't matter what type it is as long as it's a dinosaur. The fact that the Sullivans live near Rocky Mountain National Park works out great for us. If Mom and Dad had not known them, I don't think they would have let us come on this trip alone."

"You're right."

They had never met Johnson and Sarah Sullivan, but they had heard much about them. The Sullivans were friends and former neighbors of Anna's and Christian's grandparents. Over the years, they had kept in touch. Mr. Sullivan, an Irish immigrant, had made his money through investments. His holdings included diamond mines as well as several banks. The Sullivans' new vacation home was located near a popular ski resort, situated close to where the dig was currently taking place. Mr. Sullivan believed in being a philanthropist and spent his golden years traveling. The excavation site that they would be photographing was less than an hour from the Sullivans' new home.

Christian and Anna's father, an archaeologist turned world-renown photographer, had been given a chance to photograph and study the fossilized remains of a *Tyrannosaurus rex* on behalf of a creation magazine. Unfortunately, Dr. Murphy's injury would prevent him from taking part in the shoot; but he was confident that Anna and Christian were capable of tackling this assignment for him.

The dig began about six weeks before, and part of the approximately eight ton dinosaur had already been excavated. The crew was hoping it would not take too much time to reveal the entire skeleton. Weather was a critical concern, so removing the skeleton before winter was imperative.

"I just can't believe Dad's injury has caused him to miss seeing this dig in person. This is going to be awesome!" Christian beamed. "You'd better take the best pictures of your life so that Dad can see this on film."

"I'll do my best," Anna agreed.

Dr. Murphy had confidence in Anna's work. At only fifteen, Anna had already gained notoriety of her own, thanks to some recently published work in which her photographs had taken center stage. One set of photographs were taken of Christian's skydiving rescue of Carolyn Rogers. After Quincy was safely in the pilot's seat, Anna used her zoom lens to get a better look at Christian and Carolyn, and automatically began snapping pictures, practically without thought. A magazine had already purchased the photographs for future publication. Several of the pictures had been published in many nationally syndicated newspapers. Another set of photographs was being used to illustrate an article on the "Missing Link." It was the dig they had accompanied their father and archaeologist uncle on a few months ago.

Christian's expertise lay in the technical aspect of photography, modifying and downloading the pictures. Actually, he was really more interested in the archeological, or in this case, paleontological aspect of the excavation.

Anna's face was etched with concern as she said, "I hope the Sullivans have made it home from their trip to London. Do you know the details of what happened? All Mom told me was that Mrs. Sullivan's mother was sick."

"Yes, that's right. Mrs. Sullivan called Mom from her trip and mentioned that her mother, in Ireland, may have pneumonia. She was unsure if they would cut their trip to London short, and head to Ireland, instead of meeting us in Colorado."

Anna nodded. "A cold at 102 years of age can be deadly."

"Thanks for telling me, Miss First-Aid."

Anna smiled, ignoring Christian's barb about knowing first aid. This was a private joke between them.

"At any rate, Mrs. Sullivan said they would decide their destination after they discovered the extent of her mother's illness." Christian added, "I'm just thankful that Mrs. Sullivan assured Mom that we could still stay at their new home, although I would feel better if they were there, too."

"Yeah," Anna agreed. "The last thing we want is to be looked after by the hired help."

The Murphy teens were grateful that they were both homeschooled; otherwise this trip to Colorado would not have been possible. They had just begun their new school year, yet they were both ahead academically. Being homeschooled allowed them to take breaks during the year; although their mother reminded them that ahead or not, work would still need to be made up.

Of course, their seven-year old brother, Andy, had a thing or two to say about the fact that he always seemed to get left behind. He was appeased with the knowledge that their Mom needed help with the four-month old twins.

"Hey! Now that I think about it, wouldn't it be great if we had the whole house to ourselves?" Christian exclaimed.

The nicely clad young woman on the other side of Christian lowered her magazine and loudly huffed, "Please, keep it down!" After making a point to glare at the two teens, she turned back to the magazine.

Until now, the Murphys' seatmate hadn't uttered a word. Christian, a shrewd judge of character, was certain the red color of her hair and her actions were telltale signs of a quick temper.

Christian shrugged wordlessly at Anna. He turned his attention back to the computer screen displaying articles about dinosaurs and the fossil record. He was looking for information on age-dating. He was hoping his research would lead to information that would help him to prove the dinosaur, which had been discovered, was not 65-million years old.

He read bits and pieces from various articles, especially quotes by noted evolutionists, one in particular, who insisted there was no evidence against evolution, then went on to stress that bacteria had not changed significantly in over a million years. *Obviously if evolution were true bacteria should have changed through the years.* Christian thought to himself.

Yet another series of articles caught his eye. These compared the way the scientists had used fossils to date the layers of rocks. In the late 1940's the article said fossils made it possible to recognize rocks of the same age in different parts of the earth. In the late 1950's it was stated that the only way to age-date rocks was by the fossils found within the layers. In the 1970's the article went on to say that these fossils, now called *index fossils*, were often restricted to rocks in a relatively limited geological span. It further explained that the method was not foolproof:

Occasionally an organism, previously thought to be extinct, is found to be in existence. Such 'living fossils' obviously cannot function as index fossils except within the broader time span of their known existence.

Christian was not surprised by the article, and saved it

under a folder he labeled, 'circular reasoning,' and began to shut down the computer. He quickly told Anna what he had read. Both were deep in thought, wondering what they would find in Colorado, as Christian slipped his computer into its padded leather case.

Anna dug into her backpack, searching for some gum. "How much longer?" she asked.

"Another twenty minutes," Christian said, as he glanced at his watch and shifted in his seat, this time bumping into the lady beside him. "Oh, excuse me. I'm sorry. ma'am," he apologized.

The red-haired lady gave Christian a curt nod, but her dark eyes betrayed her outward calm. "The name is Katherine and that's completely all right," she answered.

Katherine immediately rose from the cramped quarters, setting her magazine down on the seat with unnecessary force. She stood there glaring at Christian for a second, while regaining her balance on her unsteady platform shoes. Looking up and down the aisle, she turned making her way toward an unsuspecting flight attendant. "Do you, or do you not, give refills on this plane?" Katherine snapped.

Christian shook his head at Katherine's tone and whispered to Anna, "Well, now she can be annoyed at someone else."

"I'll take the middle seat on our way home." Anna offered and without picking up her head, she continued to read.

Their seatmate was still several feet behind the Murphys, but was talking loud enough for them to hear. "I can't believe I forgot to take my medication! Why, should I be surprised? That's what happens when you can't even hear yourself think!"

Anna and Christian exchanged looks, knowing the comment was meant for them.

Katherine came rushing back only after being assured by the kind flight attendant that her soft drink was on the way. When the lady was a mere two-steps away, she tripped and let out a gasp. Christian caught a glimpse of Katherine as she reached for the seat next to him. Anna turned just in time to see their seatmate fall with a thud, then silence.

Chapter 4
The Waiting Game

The rude comment made moments ago was now forgotten. Unclipping their seat belts, Christian and Anna rose to help. Christian breathed a silent prayer as he and his sister slipped into the aisle.

Christian, knowing Anna's expertise in first aid, went for a flight attendant while Anna knelt down. "Are you okay, Katherine?" Anna asked, she tucked her hair behind her ears, keeping it away from her face.

"Yes! How stupid of me!" Sitting up the woman adjusted her shirt.

"What hurts?" Anna asked, while mentally going through a first aid checklist, noting a scratch on her knee.

"My knee is sore."

"Yes, thankfully it doesn't look too bad, if you . . ."

"It is bad! My knee is throbbing!" she finished with a huff.

Looking up, Anna nodded with relief seeing that

Christian had arrived with the flight attendant in tow.

The pretty, blond flight attendant with a first aid kit in hand, headed toward them. Anna glanced at her badge, which read Sally Moore.

"Are you okay?" Sally asked with compassion.

At this point Katherine was tiring of the attention, "Yes I'm all right. If this young man will help me get up," Katherine paused glancing over at Christian. "That is, if you don't mind."

"I don't mind! Here give me your hand." He gently reached down and helped her to a standing position without putting pressure on her knee. Christian helped Katherine back into her seat, moving to the window seat and allowing Anna to sit in the middle beside Katherine.

Across the aisle an elderly lady was soon calling to Sally the flight attendant, for help. Sally turned, briefly apologizing to Katherine, "I'll be right back to dress your wound." She handed the kit to Katherine.

"I can do that, if you would like." Anna smiled, as Katherine nodded in agreement. Katherine couldn't stand the sight of blood no matter how minimal. Anna dressed the scrape on Katherine's knee.

"You did a great job!" Sally said, turning back to see Anna closing the first aid kit, and handing it up to Sally.

"Thanks, I didn't mind helping." Anna said to Sally, but she was smiling at Katherine.

"I need to call ahead and arrange for you to see a doctor when we land," Sally said. She spoke with Katherine further and then excused herself heading back down the aisle.

"I really do appreciate you helping, Anna. I guess I should have thought twice about wearing these shoes." Katherine smiled.

Anna smiled as she and Christian wordlessly settled into their seats.

"I'm glad you decided to become rescue dive certified and had to take the first aid and CPR training as a prerequisite. It really came in handy," Christian said as he leaned his head back and closed his eyes before adding, "I'm glad you did it for more than a great tan."

"Well, if I remember correctly, you took the same class two years ago," Anna rejoined, her large, determined brown eyes flashing, their look lost on her relaxed brother.

Eyes still shut, Christian smiled, "Yeah, but you know how I hate the sight of blood."

Ten minutes later the pilot's voice could be heard over the intercom system. We've begun our final descent into Denver International Airport," The pilot said. He thanked them for flying with USA Jet Lines and added, "Looks like clear skies and forty degrees."

Christian opened his eyes, refreshed after his short nap, and futilely attempted to stretch his long legs. He and Anna gazed out the small window during the descent. The airport buildings grew progressively larger as the huge aircraft approached the runway. The plane seemed to speed up as it neared the black tarmac with engines thundering.

Upon landing, the plane bounced a couple of times, engines screaming in reverse as the aircraft slowed, and finally taxied to a stop. Right on time at 2:30 pm.

Christian asked Katherine if she needed help, which she declined, deciding to stay onboard until the rest of the passengers disembarked. Christian and Anna retrieved their carry-on luggage, then merged into the single-file procession heading off the plane.

The teens weren't sure who would be picking them up from the airport. One possibility was that the Sullivans would send one of their employees. If so, they expected that someone would be holding a sign with "Anna and Christian Murphy" written on it.

Emerging from the plane, Anna glanced around the terminal. She was looking for the faces memorized from the old photographs her mother had shown her of the Sullivans. The Sullivans had visited more than fifteen years ago when Anna and Christian were very young. Unfortunately, her mother didn't have more recent photos.

Christian also scanned the crowd but he saw no one who even slightly resembled the Sullivans, or anyone with a sign bearing their name. The Sullivans, both of Irish descent, had pale complexions, blue eyes, and red hair when they were younger. Their red hair probably had turned white in recent years.

Anna adjusted the straps of her teal backpack on her shoulder as she and Christian followed the others toward the baggage claim area.

Christian and Anna continued the long walk through the maze of people and chairs as they headed for the baggage claim downstairs. Once they arrived, a quick look around revealed that the Sullivans weren't there.

"Well, I wonder who's coming to pick us up?" Anna asked, still looking around, as they waited for their luggage to pass on the revolving conveyer belt. Families and friends were reuniting all around them but, oddly, they didn't feel alone.

"Mom and Dad said someone would be here when our flight landed; but, if not, we have the phone number to their house," Christian answered. "If the Sullivans come, I hope they recognize us, because I doubt we'll recognize them," he added.

"You've got that right," Anna nodded her head in agreement.

Five minutes later, Christian had scooped up his duffle bag, camera equipment, and computer case. Anna followed, carrying her duffle bag. They settled into chairs near the main doors where they could watch for their ride.

Twenty minutes later, Christian sprang from his seat and started to pace. "I wonder where they are?" he said to no one in particular. Glancing at his watch, the time revealed that it was past 3:30 pm.

Anna shrugged, giving no reply as she continued to scan the never-ending flow of people who entered and exited the terminal.

"You know, I wonder if anything has happened to them. Maybe we should call," she said standing up to stretch.

Christian stopped pacing and turned to look back at Anna, but didn't make a reply. He finally asked, "Did you say something?"

"No, I'm just talking to myself," Anna stated, giving

Christian a puzzled look.

"Hello, Anna." The voice came from behind her. Anna sighed in relief and thought, *The Sullivans have finally arrived!*

Chapter 5
Eldorado Springs, Colorado

Anna turned and instead found Katherine standing beside someone who appeared to be a real life cowboy, complete with a tall, black, cowboy hat and pointed, black cowhide boots. He stood with one muscular arm protectively draped across Katherine's shoulder.

"Hi Katherine," Anna smiled and hid her disappointment. Glancing at the large bandage on her leg Anna added, "How's your knee?"

Smiling Katherine answered, "Much better! This is my fiancé, Rick Lane. He wanted to meet you." She giggled like a schoolgirl, a complete contrast to the lady they had met earlier. She then turned to the middle-aged man. "This is the young lady I was telling you about, dear, the one who bandaged me up. She came right to my rescue when I injured my knee," Katherine explained.

"Thank you for helping my fiancée." White teeth flashed as Rick smiled down at Anna.

"Nice to meet you," Anna said, shaking his outstretched hand. Anna looked the big man over. Besides his cowboy attire, he wore a pair of faded jeans, a black waistpack, and a monogrammed blue shirt with a red logo that read "Rocky Mountain National Park."

"I see you work at the national park. Are you a ranger?" Anna asked.

Rick gave Anna a bewildered look, then with comprehension grinned. "You're a quick study. Yes, I'm a ranger, among other things."

"He works in the Historic Sites Department," Katherine interjected with pride.

Christian walked up to stand beside his sister. "Hi, Katherine, I see you're feeling better." Katherine nodded and introduced Christian to Rick, watching as they shook hands.

Rick's eyes narrowed as he read the words on Christian's T-shirt, *Believe and Achieve: Commit to the Lord whatever you do and your plans will succeed. Proverbs 16:3.*

"It's a small world," Christian said. "My sister and I are here to photograph the dinosaur fossil that is being unearthed in the park. We've been in contact with Luke Gotham. Do you know him?"

Rick folded his arms, giving Christian a once-over. His facial expression was blank, not allowing any emotion to show; yet his jaw was tense as if he was trying hard not to clench his teeth.

Christian noticed, but said nothing.

Anna also noticed the hard line of his jaw and she tried to fill the awkward silence and make small talk. "We are waiting for a ride that seems to have forgotten us—"

"I thought a Dr. Murphy or something was going to take some pictures."

"Actually, he sprained his ankle and decided that too much walking would be difficult until he recovers. He sent us instead. He did speak with Mr. Gotham, who assured us the arrangement was acceptable."

At the second mention of Luke's name, Rick's

32

expression went from annoyance to tightly controlled menace. "I think you'll have to talk to my boss, Dr. Troy Lane. He's in charge of the excavation," he huffed. "Kid photographers, huh? Any photographing will only be allowed with Troy's approval, not Luke's," Rick finished, with annoyance now evident in his voice.

"Okay," Christian said, ignoring the barb. "Then I guess we'll be in touch with him."

Rick shrugged, turned, and without a word, he grasped Katherine firmly under the elbow, and steered her away. Katherine turned back with a helpless look and waved. "Bye and thanks!" she called.

Both Murphys stood side-by-side, with Christian more than a head taller, as they watched the two figures retreat into the cold air outside the glass doors. A rapidly thickening fog had replaced the earlier clear skies.

Anna returned to her seat. "What do you make of Rick?" she asked, scooting the bags at her feet into a straight line.

"Other than as a person who can't grasp the fact that we can actually do an adult's job?" Christian asked.

"Yeah, well, you can't blame him about that. But did you notice the way he acted when we mentioned Luke Gotham?" Anna added with a puzzled expression.

"That was really obvious. I wonder what the deal is?"

"I guess we'll find out," Anna said, still studying the bags on the floor. Then she perked up. "Hey, this could be a mystery."

Christian grinned. "I bet I can solve the first part of the mystery of why Rick likes Troy."

"How can you possibly explain that?" Anna asked. "We don't even know them."

"Easy." Christian smiled knowingly. "What was Rick's last name?"

"I think he said it was Lane. So?"

Christian kept grinning. Anna still looked bewildered, so he continued, "You're right, and Troy's last name is also Lane, as in Dr. Lane."

"Oh, I get it! They're probably related! Father and son or even brothers!" Anna excitedly concluded.

Christian smiled and then nodded in agreement. "That would explain his reaction to Troy!"

Forty-five very long minutes passed when Anna finally suggested, "How about having the Sullivans paged?"

"Good idea," Christian agreed. "I'll be right back," he said over his shoulder.

The page went out three times, but no one responded. "I think we better call the house. Where's the number?" Christian asked.

Anna started rummaging through her backpack but after a few minutes came up empty handed. "I can't find it. The number was in my daytimer. I remember packing it, but it's not here!"

"Great!" Christian said, slouching further in his chair. "This means we need to call home, and the last thing we want is to have them worry about us." Christian pulled out his cell phone, but before he could dial, an older couple approached them.

A fashionably dressed, white-haired lady and a distinguished looking man, in khaki pants and crisp oxford shirt, stood in front of the two teens. "You must be Christian and Anna. How are you? We're the Sullivans." The woman declared with an Irish brogue.

Her accent was so thick, that Anna half expected the woman to do a little jig, but she shook the thought from her mind.

Christian flipped his phone closed and looked hard-pressed not to blurt out how he was *really* doing. He willed himself to recognize any resemblance of the younger woman in the photo, but he could see none.

Anna rose and stepped forward to shake hands, but instead was greeted with a bear hug. "Yes, I am Anna," she said, crushed against the woman's fur coat, silk scarf, and overpowering perfume.

"Oh, isn't she just a darling?" Mrs. Sullivan cooed.

Mr. Sullivan enthusiastically nodded a reply, while he vigorously pumped Christian's hand and gave his arm a workout. He was incredibly strong for his age. "Sorry we're late. I had to wait for Sarah to return with the car."

"I've been shopping up a storm since we've gotten here.

You know there is so much to buy when you move into a new house."

"A vacation house," Mr. Sullivan reminded her.

"Oh you know, I've just got to make it homey." Mrs. Sullivan countered good-naturedly.

Mr. Sullivan winked. "I love to spoil her."

Anna tried to disentangle herself from Mrs. Sullivan's firm grasp, and finally succeeded. Anna sympathetically asked, "How is your mother doing?"

"Oh! Bless your heart! You're a lovely girl to ask. She's doing much better, recovering from her cold nicely."

"I am so glad!"

Christian reached down to gather their luggage when Mrs. Sullivan interrupted. "Don't touch those!" she said in horror. "Where is Raphael?" she turned with impatience.

"Waiting in the double park lane," Mr. Sullivan reminded her. With an air of authority, he quickly signaled a skycap.

Their bags were promptly hoisted onto a luggage cart and whisked out the door to the waiting car before either of the teens could protest. A blast of cold air hit the four as they left the warm building.

"We're so glad you could come for a visit," Mr. Sullivan stated. Seemingly unaffected by the cold, he removed a large wad of cash from his pocket and pulled off a couple of bills for a tip.

Christian's mouth fell open in disbelief as he stared at the large, shiny, black car parked on the curb. Neither Anna nor Christian were expecting a junky car. They knew the Sullivans were wealthy. But, even with that knowledge, they certainly weren't expecting to be chauffeured in a limousine. Catching himself, Christian quickly recovered and snapped his gaping mouth shut, then exclaimed, "Nice limo!"

Anna nodded in agreement, too cold to speak. She felt as though she was frozen to the bone. "I am f . . .freezing!" Anna said through chattering teeth.

Mr. Sullivan let out a hardy laugh; "Hardly freezing! This is not cold. Maybe if you're lucky, it will snow in the mountains while you're here."

Anna shivered as she stopped to pull out an unlined London Fog jacket from her backpack. It was the thickest jacket she owned, needing little else while living in Florida. She wrapped her arms around her middle in an attempt to get warm, although it did little good.

The trunk to the limo was wide open, as the driver ran around to open the passenger doors and help them in, before attending to the luggage. The large Hispanic man accepted the money Mr. Sullivan gave him to tip the skycap. Contrary to his height and build, the dark-haired driver moved effortlessly.

Without a thought, Christian, went to the luggage cart, intending to help load the trunk.

"I'll do that," the big man politely informed him.

Christian was about to argue when Mr. Sullivan's authoritative voice boomed, "Let him do it lad. That's what he's paid to do."

Christian got into the car without further comment, but felt appalled that anyone, wealthy or not, would treat another person with such condescension.

Anna, already in the car, was sitting across from Mrs. Sullivan, and beside Christian in a rear-facing seat. Mrs. Sullivan reached over, patted her hand, and started talking a mile-a-minute. Anna quietly exchanged looks with Christian. The Sullivans, and their lifestyle, would take some getting use to.

"I can't wait for you to see the house. I am having a grand time buying little things to make it look like home. I'm just so glad to finally meet you both and have you stay with us."

"Anna and I appreciate your invitation," Christian answered Mrs. Sullivan.

Anna snapped back out of her musings, "Yes, thanks for having us."

"Someday we'd love to have your whole family out, although your Mum may want to wait to travel until the twins are older," Mrs. Sullivan said. "Oh, twins!" she gushed, "How lovely!"

With warmth surrounding her, Anna was finally able to

think. Noting that Christian was handling Mrs. Sullivan's questions, she quickly lost track of the conversation and began to study the lady who was sitting across from her. Mrs. Sullivan, at five feet eight inches, was about three inches taller than Anna. But in relation to the description her mother had provided and the photo, the only resemblance was in her eyes. The sparkling blue matched almost exactly. Anna reasoned that it had been about fifteen years; a lot of time spent out in the sun, and a few more pounds, that made Mrs. Sullivan look different from the photo. Satisfied for the moment, Anna next turned to study Mr. Sullivan, who had just seated himself next to his wife. Besides his silver hair and hollowed cheeks, he looked like an older version of the once tall and well-built man in the photo. He had an air of hardness around his eyes, but his friendly smile, impeccable dress, and flashy gold wristwatch seemed to downplay this notion. The turn of conversation brought Anna out of her reflection.

"Is anyone hungry?" Mrs. Sullivan asked.

Anna opened her mouth to reply, but Christian beat her. "I am," he quickly announced.

"Me too," Anna grinned.

"We've planned a big dinner back at our house. We usually dress in formal attire for dinner, but casual is fine for tonight," Mr. Sullivan stated, leaning back comfortably in the plush, leather seat. He pushed a button on his cell phone. "I'll make sure dinner is ready soon after we arrive."

Formal dress for dinner; he has got to be kidding! Christian thought, yet forced a smile to his face and said, "That sounds great."

"I simply must go shopping for you sometime soon. Maybe tomorrow!" Mrs. Sullivan exclaimed glancing at Anna. "You'll need a coat and some sweaters."

Anna looked at Christian, answering for them both, "A warmer jacket would be nice. We have spending money—"

"Now, I won't hear of that," Mr. Sullivan interrupted his conversation on the cell phone to interject. "You're our guests."

"But—" Anna tried feebly to argue, knowing her mother wouldn't be pleased to impose on the Sullivans' generosity.

37

"Warm clothes sound good to me too, before Anna and I freeze," Christian interrupted, silencing Anna with a glance. They could argue the point of who would pay later.

Mr. Sullivan ended his conversation and then clipped the cell phone to the waistband of his pants. As he followed their gazes to the scenic mountain range he warned, "This is beautiful country, but rugged. You've got to be a survivor to make it out here. You both need to watch yourselves. Understand?"

"We'll be careful," Anna said, though she wasn't sure what he meant.

"We have a small staff in place. It is half the size of the staff of our other homes. If you need anything at all, and we are not available, just ask for Cindy or Sam Norris. We sent them ahead before we moved in. They are the managers of this new home. They came ahead and hired the staff and are very capable. They run things so smoothly that they only work part time. Do you have any questions?" Mrs. Sullivan asked.

Anna and Christian shook their heads.

"Well, Sarah and I both want you to make yourselves at home, but we are busy people . . . what with financial matters and all . . ." Mr. Sullivan trailed off, seemingly uncomfortable talking about his philanthropic efforts.

"We don't want to be a burden," Christian said. "We plan to camp out at the national park several nights."

"My goodness, that's not what he meant," Mrs. Sullivan cooed. "He just wants you two to have free reign of the house, and not worry about what we are doing or checking with us over every little detail or places you want to go. You know we just arrived ourselves."

"I'm sure you have to check with your parents at home about going out. Well not here! Just leave us a note, or tell the help, and you can come and go as you please." Mr. Sullivan announced smiling broadly as if they had won the grand prize in a drawing.

Christian and Anna were speechless. Not that they lived in a prison, but their parents were adamant that they must know at all times where they were, especially once Christian had obtained his driver's license. This freedom was contrary to years of training.

"Oh, thank you." Anna answered, while Christian was still too shocked to speak.

Recovering too late to add anything to the conversation, Christian turned his attention out the window. He was amazed to see that few other vehicles were on the road once they exited busy US Highway 36 toward Eldorado Springs. They were currently traveling down the single, large thoroughfare, running through the center of the popular ski resort town.

The foursome grew quiet, allowing the heat from the warm interior to relax them. The enjoyable, peaceful minute lasted just that . . . a minute.

Suddenly the limo driver slammed on the brakes and cranked the wheel to the left. The back end slid around, and the limo narrowly missed hitting a red 4x4 that had run a red light. Unfortunately, the fog had cast a thin layer of moisture on the streets, and the sharp turn sent the limo into a deadly spin in the middle of the intersection.

The four passengers froze as the limo started to swerve out of control. Anna and Christian were pushed against the taut seat belts as they gazed out of the tinted windows in terror.

Chapter 6
No Place Like This Home

With the horn blaring, the 4x4 didn't slow, and zoomed out of sight. The limo careened down the street. Traffic going both ways managed to barely avoid hitting the long black car as it passed. The fog did little good to help the driver get his bearings.

Mrs. Sullivan, who had been stunned with fear, now let out a high-pitched scream. "Help! Somebody do something!" she breathlessly gasped.

The car finally screeched to a halt.

"What the—" Mrs. Sullivan abruptly stopped, seeming to catch herself, as she clutched onto Mr. Sullivan's arm.

The car finally stopped, blocking the two lanes of traffic. Anna was struggling to control her fears, as horns continued to blare, yet couldn't help looking at Mrs. Sullivan with surprise. What had happened to her Irish accent so evident moments earlier? Anna nudged Christian with her knee, but he was enthralled with the happenings outside the window of the limo.

"Is everyone okay?" Raphael's voice was heard over the speakers.

"Yes, we're just fine," Mr. Sullivan replied.

Satisfied, Raphael emerged from the limo and quickly started to direct the traffic around his vehicle. Once the traffic lightened, he jumped back in and expertly navigated the limo back onto the road. They were back on their way once again.

"Did you hear that?" Anna hissed.

"What?" Christian asked, puzzled.

"Never mind, I'll tell you later," she whispered.

"Is everyone all right?" Mr. Sullivan asked, looking at Anna and Christian while patting his wife's hand. "It's all right, my beauty, it's all right."

Anna and Christian nodded. "We're fine."

Anna looked puzzled. Mr. Sullivan's accent was firmly in place and Mrs. Sullivan, her face strained, remained looking out of the window in silence. Maybe she just imagined it.

"I think you'll like the house, it's a bit rugged, but we think it matches this area. We had it built on the top of a small mountain overlooking a lake. It's a beauty," Mr. Sullivan said, still patting Sarah's hand comfortingly. "We'll be there shortly."

"I can't wait to see it. I understand you have several homes," Christian said.

"Yes, we like to travel, but we don't enjoy staying in hotels. Instead, we have homes built in places that appeal to us. But I must say we still consider Ireland our real home."

"How many homes do you have?" Anna blurted out without thinking.

"Four or five... can't keep track," Mr. Sullivan laughed. Yet the smile didn't quite reach his eyes. "I'm getting on in years, and can't remember everything."

"Oh, I didn't mean to pry." Anna felt foolish for asking.

"Not at all, not at all. Look now; we're at the gate," Mr. Sullivan waved out the window as they approached an imposing metal gate. It slowly opened as the limo pulled up to the asphalt drive.

The beautifully landscaped entrance took Anna's and

Christian's breath away. The tree-lined driveway consisted of tall aspens and large stately oak trees that could be seen at a distance. The shrubs were well trimmed and colorful plants dotted the brick- bordered driveway.

The house could not be seen from the road, which made it even more private. After finally reaching the structure, the teens were amazed. Several buildings of various widths and heights were staggered to make up the Sullivans' large residence. The cedar and brick buildings were joined by wooden boardwalks, overhangs, and surrounding decks. The limo slid to a halt under the large, covered portico. Immense cedar posts held up the imposing roof structure, which contained recessed lighting. Built into the base of each of the posts, planters flowed with flowers intermixed with evergreens shrubs. Anna and Christian were anxious to step out of the limo; but, they managed to wait until Raphael came around to open the door. A glance between both teens confirmed they were thinking the same thing, once again. This would definitely take some time to become accustomed to.

Mr. and Mrs. Sullivan stepped out, at ease as several people greeted them. Soon there was a flurry of activity. Suitcases were lifted out of the trunk and packages, from earlier purchases made by the Sullivans, were carted into the house.

Floor-to-ceiling glass seemed to greet Anna and Christian everywhere they looked. The double-paned glass doors were trimmed in oak; but, Anna was able to see into the house without them being opened. Anna pulled out her 35 mm camera from her backpack as she stepped out of the limo door held open by Raphael. He reached in and gave her a hand.

"Thank you," she said.

Raphael, caught off-guard by her kind words, mumbled, "You're welcome."

Though gratitude was automatic to Anna, Raphael was not accustomed to it. He had apparently worked for few people, who took the time to thank him. The Sullivans all but ignored him.

After briefly examining the landscape with a critical eye, Anna took several pictures of the front lawn and then one picture of the house.

"Hey!" Mr. Sullivan hollered with alarm as he turned to find Anna in the act.

"Excuse me?" Anna asked. Startled by his tone. She lowered her camera.

Mr. Sullivan's steely voice demanded an answer, "You're taking pictures?" he thundered.

Too surprised to answer, Anna stared at him speechlessly.

"Anna loves photography, and you remember the reason for our visit, don't you? To take pictures," Christian explained for Anna.

"Ah, yes . . . I er, forgot," Mr. Sullivan responded faintly laughing. "Remember, I told you I was forgetful."

"Oh my dear, you know, we hate to have our own pictures taken ... you understand?" Mrs. Sullivan laughed, trying to clarify what Johnson meant as she looked from Christian to Anna. "Nobody likes the way they look in pictures!" She smiled.

"Yes, you are right about that," Christian answered, ruefully remembering the many times Anna had taken pictures of him at awkward moments.

"If you promise not to take any pictures of us personally, then snap away." Mrs. Sullivan waved her hands as if dismissing them. Walking away, she took Johnson's arm and with a slight tug led him to the door.

Anna stared in disbelief. *I thought the rich, and famous loved to have their pictures taken.*

Raphael approached the open trunk to help the others with the packages. Christian came around at the same time, hoping to be of assistance.

"It's not necessary for you to help; we can get them." Raphael glanced over his shoulder worriedly in the direction of the older couple, who were making their way to the entrance. He made sure he wouldn't be overheard before saying, "Sam and Cindy are the ones who should be here to help, but are never around when you need them. They're the managers and work part time, you know, but they might as well be no time."

"But I don't mind helping. Anna doesn't pack light,

44

especially with all the photography equipment, and . . . whew!" Christian gave a low whistle, "They weren't kidding about shopping!" Packages and shopping bags sporting name brands lined the trunk area. The Sullivans, it appeared, had even paid a visit to a jewelry store.

"Christian, come on! Raphael and the others can get it all," Mr. Sullivan hollered. "I want you to meet the staff."

Christian stubbornly shouldered his computer case, picked up his duffel bag, and followed in Mr. Sullivan's direction.

He joined Anna in the entryway. Honey oak floors gleamed underfoot, and they seemed to be an extension of the outdoors. The massive foyer was framed with high, open beams, curved stairs led upward on either side of the entryway. Directly in front, the sunken living area sported a round fireplace in the center. Floor-to-ceiling windows revealed a breathtaking view of the sparkling lake and mountains in the background.

"Welcome to our abode!" Mrs. Sullivan announced with a flourish. She stood in the middle of the huge room apparently waiting for something to happen.

"This is awesome!" Anna gasped.

Three people quickly made their way into the room. A butler moved aside to make room for the two women; the group of three formed a prim line. Both women wore spotless white aprons over black dresses. "Hilary, Susan, and Mitch, meet Anna and Christian Murphy."

"Nice to meet you," they said in unison. Anna half expected the women to curtsy and Mitch to bow.

"Hilary is our cook; Susan the maid; and Mitch the butler, handy man, and whatever. Sam and Cindy are off today. Being managers they are working behind the scenes so to speak." Mrs. Sullivan motioned to the cook and said, "We'll expect dinner in thirty minutes."

"Yes, ma'am."

Mr. Sullivan, deep in thought, missed the introductions. "Did you introduce the staff Sarah?"

"Yes. My goodness Johnson, you're surely not thinking about your charitable work so soon?"

"Yes, well, there is much to be done."

"Excuse me, sir, there is someone waiting for you in the study. It's Mr. Richard L—"

"Mitch, take my coat!" Mrs. Sullivan snapped with annoyance cutting him off.

Mitch seemed to flinch at the sound of her voice. "Yes, ma'am!"

"I'll be in my study." Mr. Sullivan said as he entered a large room to the right of the foyer, shutting the door behind him.

As Mitch was helping Mrs. Sullivan out of her fur coat, she spoke to Susan. "Show the kids to their rooms. I'm going to change."

"Yes, Mrs. Sullivan," Susan said.

Mrs. Sullivan left without a backward glance, leaving only the clinking sound of her heels connecting with the wood stairs as she spryly climbed to the second floor.

Anna and Christian had little choice but to stand in the middle of the huge room and wait until Susan showed them the way. They felt totally out of place.

"Come this way, please. Most of the luggage is already in your rooms." Susan gave a sideward glance at Christian, who still carried his computer case and duffle bag. She motioned for them to follow as she headed up to the second floor. Instead of following Mrs. Sullivan to the right, she turned left.

The threesome made their way up the stairs and down the hall with Susan in the lead and Christian bringing up the rear. Christian stopped walking and stepped up to the railing to peer down to the foyer below. The only sound that could be heard was their shoes as they walked on the oak flooring. Christian was sure that if he dropped a pin, the sound would be deafening in the beautiful, but cold, house.

"Here are your rooms. There are two separate entries to each of your bedrooms, and they join in the middle," Susan showed Anna and Christian, as she pointed to two doors separated by a large curved wall. She walked into Anna's room and said, "Lights on." The room immediately brightened. "The lighting works on voice command or regular switches on the wall."

"Wow! This is unbelievable," Christian greeted Anna in the middle room after he had deposited his bags in the adjoining bedroom. He walked over to where Susan and his sister stood. The two bedrooms led to an enormous living room area, and all three rooms were shaped in a semicircle. Once again, floor-to-ceiling windows afforded them with a view of the lake and mountains. Stepping out onto the private balcony, Christian and Anna could see lights beginning to twinkle in the distance.

After closing the French doors, Susan said, "This is your entertainment center." She pushed a button on a remote control, and the picture on the wall receded into the ceiling. An entertainment center, complete with a flat-screened television hanging from the wall; a sound system, and disk players were each recessed into wall cabinets. "There is even a karaoke if you are so inclined," Susan finished.

Anna put her camera case down on the couch, "Thank you. It's kind of you to show us around."

"It's my pleasure, Miss Murphy." The maid's smile was forced.

"Please, won't you call me Anna?"

Susan looked surprised. "I'm not sure if Mrs. Sullivan would approve."

"Oh, please," Anna persisted.

This time when the young woman smiled it was genuine, "Well, if you insist."

"Look, Anna, a popcorn machine, like at the movies!" Christian grinned.

"There is also a stocked refrigerator underneath the bar with sodas and snacks."

"Wow, this is great. Thanks!"

"Would you like me to unpack?" Susan politely inquired.

Anna smiled, but shook her head, "No, thanks." "Okay then, if there is anything you need, just press number two on the phone. You will reach me directly," Susan said, pointing to a cell phone attached to the waistband of her apron.

Anna was uncomfortable asking Susan for anything she

could get herself. "I think we'll be fine. Thanks."

"Dinner will be in fifteen minutes," Susan announced. "The Sullivans normally dress formally for dinner, but asked that you dress casually tonight. Are you sure I can't help you unpack?"

"No thanks, Susan," Anna hesitated, "We didn't really bring dressy clothes."

"I'm sure the Sullivans will assist you in purchasing whatever you need. They are always shopping." Having said that, Susan looked around nervously as though she'd said too much.

"Well, thanks. We'll see you downstairs." Christian frowned, unsure of what he would wear for a dressy occasion.

The door shut gently as Susan hurried off to help with the meal.

"Can you believe this?" Anna asked. "I mean, look at this place!" She gestured to the entertainment center in wonder.

"I'm still stuck on the formal dress for dinner requirement! All I brought were denim jeans and one nice pair of pants for church!" Christian said.

"Oh, let's not worry about it! I want to check out our rooms." Anna turned into her bedroom once again. Her room was beautifully decorated with a queen-size brass bed with an authentic quilt, matching polished redwood furniture, and plush white carpeting. Christian's room was similarly furnished, but with deep blue carpeting. Their duffle bags were on racks, ready for unpacking.

Anna began to unzip her duffle bag and hang her only dress, ruefully wishing she had brought more. Christian sat on the ottoman next to the balcony window.

"What was the deal in the limo?" Christian asked, referring to when Anna had kneed him.

Anna took a deep breath before answering, "I could swear I heard Mrs. Sullivan lose her accent."

"What? You've got to be kidding. People just don't lose accents."

"I'm not. When the limo began to skid, she started screaming."

48

"Yeah, so? I remember that part."

"Well, she said a few words with her accent intact, but then she said . . . 'What the' . . . In those few words, it was as though she lost her accent, and she actually sounded like she was from the Bronx."

"The Bronx? Are you sure?"

"No, I'm not sure. But I think we need to keep our eyes and ears open."

"For what? Bossy friends of our grandparents with fake Irish accents?"

"Okay, so that does sound silly," Anna admitted with a shrug. "But something just doesn't..."

"I'm going to the balcony. I want to see the view again," Christian said.

Anna didn't answer. She continued to unpack, replaying the words she heard. *Yes, I'm sure Mrs. Sullivan sounded anything but Irish, but so what? Did that mean anything?*

Breaking through her musing, Anna heard Christian yelling, "Anna! Come here! You're not going to believe this!"

"What now? Five flavors of popcorn can be made at once?" she asked jokingly, wondering if Christian was trying the popcorn maker.

Anna walked out of her room and onto the balcony beside her brother. Her mouth dropped open in surprise. In the distant sky, she could just barely see the outline of a man, and he appeared to be... flying!

Chapter 7
Flying High

The next morning dawned with temperatures hovering in the upper forties. It was a lot colder than Florida; yet, Anna and Christian were enjoying breakfast on the first floor deck. The view of the lake and mountains was breathtaking. The deck rested on pillars and extended over the water. Anna and Christian felt as if they sat on a floating island. The Sullivans had already left for the day.

"If yesterday was any indication of how the rest of the trip is going to be, we're in for some adventure!" Anna said savoring the fresh fruit salad in front of her. "I can't believe that hang glider we saw last evening! I guess that's how the rich and famous live around here."

"It's strange that the Sullivans had never seen that hang glider before," Christian added. During dinner the previous evening, they all had been entertained by the antics of a man, who while gliding in a sitting position, was able to speed up, slow down, and turn in great arcs across the sky. This event could be seen just about everywhere in the house because each major room had a balcony with a view of the lake, and the formal dining room was no exception.

"The Sullivans haven't been here very long, so they probably don't know the neighbors too well, if it was a neighbor." Christian helped himself to another, freshly baked muffin, and scrambled eggs. "I'm just glad there is no, what is it called? Sorbet between courses for breakfast."

They had enjoyed a banquet for dinner. After each course, sorbet, a sherbert-type dessert, was served. The Sullivans had explained that it was used to cleanse the pallet before the next course was served.

"I love sorbet, but you're right, eating dessert before the end of a meal is different!"

They both laughed.

"I just don't know what to make of the Sullivans. They are obviously very generous," Anna said, pointing to the brightly colored wool pullover ski sweaters both she and Christian were wearing. After dinner, they found packages in the adjoining living area, with warm clothes for both of them to wear. The Sullivans obviously had sent someone shopping to buy clothing soon after their guests' arrival.

"I just wish the Sullivans had given us some guidelines. What if we decide to go to the dig and they have other plans for us?" Anna asked.

"It seems they're not expecting us to do anything with them during a set time. And you won't believe what Sam, the staff manager, gave me this morning." Christian held up a small, white envelope, handing it to Anna.

She opened the flap, looked in, and then poured out the contents: two keys and a pair of keyless entry devices hung on a single ring. "Car keys?"

"Yes, there was a note attached that said they were for the Porsche and the Hummer. We can use either car we wish. We now have our own transportation to get to the dig and back."

"Right. Quit joking, Christian."

"I'm serious!" Christian smiled at the look of disbelief on Anna's face. "What? You were expecting the limo?"

"I don't know what I was expecting, definitely nothing that has happened so far. Well, I'll make sure to take a picture of you driving a Porsche and a Hummer! Our friends will never believe it! You, in a Porsche," Anna said shaking her head and smiling.

"Yeah, well, I think the Hummer would be a more practical choice for an paleontological dig. We need to get busy and make plans for the week," Christian said, opening a green three-ring binder full of information about the dig. Christian pointed to his notebook, which was opened to a drawing of the dig. "Have you had a chance to read it?"

"Not really, I just know what Dad told us." Anna recited, "The dinosaur is a *T. rex*. It's been dated at millions of years, which we know is bogus. The main problem is the dig is extremely remote and difficult to get to. And something about the bones being found by hikers a few months ago."

"Right on all accounts," Christian nodded approval. "Several students from Colorado State University discovered the fossils while rappelling during their summer vacation. They were standing on a ledge, which, as far as I can tell from these drawings, is somewhat protected. The mountainside has a protruding, cove-shape ledge. The report states the bones appear to be of an entire dinosaur rather than bits and pieces," Christian pointed out. "Not many *T. rexes* have been found intact."

"Is the university in charge of the dig because some of the students found the fossil?" Anna asked.

"Yes, the students shared the information with one of their professors. After checking it out, he applied for permission to dig. The paleontologist, currently in charge of the dig, was once the department head at the school. He had spent the last six weeks working on this excavation with funding coming mostly from the university and private donors."

"I'm surprised a national park is allowing an excavation to take place, what with protecting and preserving the environment and all," Anna stated.

Christian looked surprised. Anna smiled, shrugging her shoulders, "I do listen when you and Dad talk about this stuff, more than you think."

"Well, you're right; it is difficult to get permission, unless the find is of substantial worth. Especially when paleontologists want to use dynamite to blast away sections of rock to save time, which they are definitely not allowed to do on this dig! They received a permit through the Bureau of Land Management since it is on Federal land. There is one more thing we need to consider so we can plan a strategy. We may have some problems with the man in charge, an evolutionist. Dr. Troy Lane is not exactly happy to know a creation magazine wants pictures of the dig."

"Yes, but didn't Dad say a creationist is also working on this dig?"

"Yeah, a man named Luke Gotham," Christian flipped through his notes, "He is also a professor at the university, but happens to be a Christian that believes in creation."

"That's a relief, especially if we will be spending several days at the dig. So what do you think? Should we drive out today, look around, and then ask permission to set up a time to take pictures?"

"That sounds great, but first I need to call Dr. Lane. The only number I have is a cell phone number. I have directions to Rocky Mountain National Park, which is only about a forty-five minute drive from here. Unfortunately, the directions get vague once we're there, and the park is huge. I don't want to go hiking around trying to find this dig. It appears to be off the beaten path." Christian finished the last of his muffin. "That was a great meal!" he sighed.

"You say that about every meal!" Anna chuckled. "Well, hurry and call; I'm ready to get going. I don't feel right about wandering around the house without the Sullivans here."

"Why do you say that?" Christian paused from dialing his cell phone to look at Anna.

"Well, if you must know, I feel a bit guilty." Anna quickly launched into an explanation. "I took a wrong turn this morning trying to find my way down for breakfast. I found myself in the other wing of the house, still on the second floor. A bedroom door was opened and I walked past glancing in. There was a large dressing table with an enormous selection of wigs."

"So?" Christian demanded. "Did you walk in and try one on?"

"Ha! Very funny," Anna said, "I just feel like there are a bunch of questions and I don't have the answers. Does that make sense?"

"No."

"Come on Christian! Think about it! What responsible adults leave two kids alone with a multimillion dollar house, and cars?" The sudden roar of an engine drowned her last words and effectively ended the conversation.

"Watch out below!" bellowed a voice from above.

The Murphys watched in disbelief as a helmeted man landed on the deck and, unable to stop, continued at full speed toward them. The crash was unavoidable.

The man collided with the table, sending the plates and food in all directions. The teens instinctively pushed away from the table and were sent sprawling to the deck. Then, a parachute covered them completely.

"I'm sorry!" a muffled, disembodied voice apologized. "I misjudged the landing."

"Anna, are you okay?" Christian asked as he tried to crawl out from under the parachute. Being a skydiver, he knew better than to stand, but Anna was becoming more entangled as she tried to stand, flailing her arms and blindly trying to find her way out.

"I'm fine, but this thing is huge. How do you get out?" she demanded.

"Drop to your knees and crawl," the muffled voice replied.

Christian found the edge and freed himself from the parachute, then helped Anna out. A big hump sat in the middle, unmoving.

"Are you okay, sir?" Christian asked.

55

"Yeah, can you help me out? I'm kinda stuck." A muffled laugh responded.

Christian bundled the chute up as he walked to the huddled form in the middle. He couldn't believe his eyes. A thin man sat stiff legged in the middle wearing protective knee and elbow pads. His helmet had fallen over his face, causing his voice to become muffled. His hands were hopelessly entangled in the parachute lines. Also incredible was the fan strapped to his back!

"Here, let me help you with that." Christian unclipped the helmet and removed it from the man's head.

"What a ride! Thanks, man!" said a young Asian American, no older than Christian. He smiled from behind laughing black eyes. "And thanks for calling me sir! Such polite neighbors."

"You could have been killed!" Anna cried rubbing her hip, which she knew would later sport a bruise, from bumping it on the table. She did not appreciate the humor of the situation.

"Nah, I've done this lots of times. It's great! I just ran out of gas, so I needed to land somewhere quickly. Actually I wasn't in any danger. This parachute allows me to glide down anywhere!"

Christian continued the process of untangling their uninvited guest, and smiled despite himself. "Hi, I'm Christian Murphy and this is my sister Anna."

"The name is Song Le, Scott Song Le."

Give me a break, Anna thought. *He thinks he's James Bond!*

"Do you live here?" Scott asked. "I thought the people who built this house were elderly."

"We are visiting the owners, friends of our grandparents," Anna supplied, still unimpressed with Scott. She glanced at him as she began picking up the spilled food. On closer inspection, she liked his infectious smile. He had laughing, slanting black eyes, and short, jet-black hair parted on the side.

"What is this contraption?" Christian asked. Unlike his sister, Christian wanted to know all about it. He would love to take a ride, himself. Of course, now was not the time to bring it up.

"Isn't it great! It's a Song Glider."

"A what?"

"You know, my last name is Song Le... and we shortened it to 'Song.' This is a paraglider. It's sort of like hang gliding, skydiving and flying all in one. Isn't it a great innovation? My Dad's an inventor."

"Awesome! Was it you we saw flying around yesterday evening?"

Anna rolled her eyes at Christian's enthusiasm as she continued to clean up.

"Actually, it was my father. He is a little better at flying this thing than I am. But I'm learning!" Scott said.

"Anna! Christian! Are you all right?" Susan came running out to the deck and viewed the mess. One look at Scott and she understood.

"Hi, Susan!" Scott grinned.

"Yes, I see you, Mr. Scott. If you weren't so cute, I would have your hide right here! Does your Dad know where you are?"

Scott just laughed.

"I see you know each other," Christian broke in.

"Yes, I used to clean for Mr. and Mrs. Song Le. But, it is a crazy house over there, and I could never keep up. Please, Anna, leave it."

"Oh I don't mind helping Susan," Anna said, "after all we don't have maids at my house!"

"No, you don't understand," Susan said, glancing over her shoulder nervously; "I would be in trouble if the Sullivans found out."

"I thought they went out."

"Yes, well they did. But they seem to know everything that goes on around here whether or not they're here. I'll come back to clean. Please leave everything where it is." Susan hurriedly left.

"Of course they know everything that goes on around the house," Scott said, smiling. "This is a 'smart' house."

"A smart house?" Christian asked.

"You know, electronically engineered with computer surveillance. The computer can be set up to store imagery that can be accessed at a later time and reviewed," Scott supplied. "My Dad makes some of the circuitry used in this house and those like it. This is similar to technology that has been used in banks and convenience stores for years," Scott said proudly.

"I still don't understand how a house can be smart." Anna said suspiciously.

"It has to do with electronics. There are motion detectors built into the light switches and stationed in the walls. You can see them if you know what to look for; they aren't hidden. When you walk in, lights turn on. Some rooms are wired to respond to voice commands," Scott explained. One hand was finally freed, and he began to unlatch the fan from the shoulder harness as Christian continued to work on the remaining tangled arm.

"Why would anyone want computer surveillance?" Anna asked.

"Are you kidding?" Scott for once looked serious, as if Anna had asked the question jokingly. Seeing her set jaw, he continued, "To deter thieves is a good reason. You see most of these homes report to a security company. So if there were an intruder, the police would be secretly notified. Others like it for the convenience of entering a room and saying, 'lights on' instead of having to physically turn them on with a switch."

"That makes sense; our bedroom lights work on voice commands," Christian enthusiastically said, loving the idea of a room that adhered to commands. "There. You're all clear."

"Thanks." Scott held out his hand and shook Christian's hand. "I appreciate it. Usually my landings are less dramatic. Would you like to try the glider sometime?"

"That would be great!" Christian answered, smiling in response.

"How did I know you would say that?" Anna replied, beginning to smile. There was something about Scott's boyish enthusiasm that was contagious.

"Is this a fan?" Christian asked with interest.

"It does look like one in design, but it's actually an air-cooled, two-cycle one-cylinder engine." Scott pointed to the contraption now lying on the floor. "This technology is quite advanced. You just run a few feet to gain momentum for flight and then up you go! The nylon canopy can be steered right or left by using a single hand control." He finished with satisfaction.

"How long can you fly without refueling?" Anna wondered out loud.

Scott turned to smile at her, then answered, "Usually about five hours; I didn't bother to refuel on purpose." He added, "I wanted to see how it would handle on a forced landing."

"You do live on the edge!" Christian shook his head then asked, "How heavy is it?"

"Only about fifty-one pounds, but the harness is especially designed to evenly distribute the weight." Scott, now standing and beginning to remove his outer pads, asked, "So, how long are you staying?"

"For two weeks. Anna is going to photograph the dinosaur dig at the Rocky Mountain National Park," Christian supplied.

"Awesome." It was Scott's turn to be impressed. "They won't let anyone near the site. How did you get permission?"

The Murphys quickly filled Scott in. "In fact, we are heading there this morning," Anna added, not wanting to be rude but anxious to be on their way.

"I can't wait to tell Kayla. She's my sister, and I think she's about your age, Anna. Sixteen, right? Her idea of a great Saturday morning is to sleep in until noon and shop the rest of the day with friends," Scott said.

"Actually, Christian is sixteen and I'm fifteen. Maybe we can meet her later on. We do need to get going," Anna smiled. Secretly, she didn't think she would have much in common with Kayla.

"How about meeting sometime this week for lunch?" Scott asked.

"Thanks, but it depends on our schedule," Anna said.

"Do you need a ride home?" Christian offered.

"No thanks, I'll call my Dad, and he'll come and get me."

"Are you sure we can't give you a ride?" Christian offered. "Do you live nearby?"

"Yeah, I live next door about a mile that way," Scott said, pointing to the north toward the lake. "No thanks about the ride; Dad will pick me up by boat. He's out running some tests on a new aerodynamic design that can cut fuel costs."

Christian's eyes sparkled. He couldn't wait to meet Scott's father. "He sounds like my kind of guy!"

Anna wasn't certain she wanted to meet any more members of the Song Le family. She was pretty sure that they wouldn't see much of each other since Scott and Kayla were probably in school. "Do you go to school around here?" she questioned.

"Yeah, Kayla attends an all-girls prep school, but I've already graduated from college." For once Scott seemed uncomfortable and almost sullen about revealing this information. "I'm taking a year off." He abruptly ended the conversation, his kind demeanor almost diminished. Turning, he unclipped a cell phone and made a call to his father. This effectively cut off any further conversation.

The Murphys exchanged puzzled glances. They were unsure of why the question seemed to bother Scott so much. "Let's go," Anna hissed, not wanting to disturb Scott as he was trying to explain his situation to his father. From the one-sided conversation, it appeared that Scott might be in more trouble than he cared to reveal.

Chapter 8
Tyrannosaurus rex!

Later that morning, the Hummer hugged the winding roads which led to one of the entrances to Rocky Mountain National Park. "I sure could get used to this!" Christian exclaimed, with one hand on the steering wheel of the powerful vehicle, while the other adjusted the visor to block the streaming sunlight. Even though the trip had taken forty minutes, Christian was enjoying every bit of driving in the all-terrain vehicle.

"Just keep both hands on the wheel," Anna said, not totally comfortable with the view. As they approached the park, the winding road appeared to be cut out of the side of the mountain. Often on either side of the extra-wide vehicle, a narrow strip of grass was the only thing between the road and the edge of the mountain. "I don't like the sheer drop on my side of the window. Don't you think they should have guard rails?"

"Maybe, but you have to admit this is a great ride."

The Hummer, not known for its fluent suspension, bounced along increasing Anna's feeling of uneasiness.

"This is nothing like the flatlands we are used to," Christian said, referring to southwest Florida's landscape. "But, you've got to agree; this is awesome."

"If Dad was driving, I'd agree. No offense," Anna said, adjusting the leather seat for the umpteenth time. She wasn't as impressed with the Hummer as Christian.

Christian glanced sideways at his sister but didn't comment. He placed both hands on the wheel to ease Anna's nervousness. At least he was enjoying the panoramic view. Sheer drops interspersed with ledges filled with thousands of trees, made the mountainous terrain on Trail Ridge Road spectacular. The leaves of the oaks, maples, and poplar trees were still green, but there was a hint of change in the colors as the teens ascended to the higher elevation.

They were expecting to meet Luke Gotham, the number-two man in charge, at the park entrance. The dig was off the beaten track, and the Murphys couldn't expect to find it without a guide at least this first time.

"It shouldn't be much longer," Christian assured his sister.

"Good," Anna said, looking straight ahead, starting to enjoy the view in spite of herself. She took several shots out the front windshield with her camera.

"Have you finished Dad's report?" Christian asked, seeing the binder on the floor at Anna's feet.

"No, I can't read it. These winding roads make me carsick. Besides, my ears keep popping like when we were on the plane."

Christian frowned slightly. "Mine too," he answered.

They spent the rest of the trip in silence, each deep in their own thoughts. A phone call had been placed to their parents soon after they were underway. Their father was not home. He was recovering from his fall, and his ankle was still sore. He had left to photograph a beached whale on the East Coast. Although rare, from time to time and for no apparent reason, they could be found beaching. Their mother was pleased to hear details of the Sullivans' amazing home, yet she was disappointed their hosts had not been home earlier when she'd called. She wanted to thank them for their hospitality. Somehow it didn't seem right to tell their mother that the guardians they had been entrusted to wanted the teenagers to enjoy themselves without any chaperones. Christian ended the call with a promise to keep in touch.

"I wonder what Mom would say if she knew the Sullivans were letting us do whatever we wanted?" Anna thought aloud.

"I don't think she'd be too happy, but she does trust us," Christian said. "Hey, look. There's the sign for the park entrance. We're almost there."

Christian followed signs to the Rocky Mountain National Park from the city of Estes Park. After paying the fee at the Beaver Meadows entrance, he drove south and pulled into the Longs Peak Ranger Station and campgrounds.

"Hey, look – the sign says we're at 9,500 feet. The air does feel a bit thinner, doesn't it?" Anna asked.

"Yeah. Sometimes I have to take an extra, deep breath, but so far it's not too bad. Come on. Let's see if Mr. Gotham is here," Christian said.

Anna was happy to unbuckle and jump out of her seat. "Oh it's gorgeous!" She raved, finally enjoying the view. Gigantic pines, oaks, and aspen trees lined the drive, giving a sense of a great span of time. "Our trees aren't nearly this big at home," Anna said. She was awed by their immense size.

"That's because of our hurricanes. Our pine trees don't get to grow this tall," Christian said with a smile; "besides, we don't often see aspens, or the same types of oaks. Ours are mostly scrub oaks."

"And, those are ugly in comparison to these," Anna commented, as she focused and snapped another picture.

She took one photo of the rustic ranger station and then another of the distant mountains and trees. The parking lot was dotted with a few vehicles. The campgrounds and ranger station were across from each other. Anna took out her camera and captured the antics of a gray squirrel chasing a bird and ended with a shot of the sun streaming through the foliage of a large aspen tree.

"You must be the Murphys." A tall, well built man in his mid-thirties greeted them. "I'm Luke Gotham. Nice shirt." He read the words out loud, "Jammin' for Jesus, whatever your hand finds to do, do it with all your might... Eccl. 9:10."

"Thanks," Christian smiled. "So how did you know it was us, Mr. Gotham?" Christian asked, his hand outstretched to shake Luke's hand.

"Just a hunch," he grinned. "Please, call me Luke."

Anna smiled knowingly, "Could the fact that Christian told you we would be arriving in a white Hummer have helped?"

Laugh lines were evident as Luke's blue eyes crinkled. "Yes, that did come in handy." He immediately became serious. "I need to warn you I have some ground rules. Watch yourselves out here and don't travel alone. There have been several ... um ... instances where pranks have been played around the dig site and the entire park for that matter. Some things have been missing, and a mountain man of sorts is being blamed. His name is Lawrence Edelman."

"Do they have any proof?" Christian asked.

"Yes, he leaves a yellow buttercup, which is a poisonous flower, as a sign."

"Is he dangerous?" Anna asked.

"Not really. He's a tree hugger—you know— save the trees. I don't think he is too happy about us whacking his precious mountain with pickaxes. Not that I think we shouldn't want to protect the environment, but this is a once-in-a-lifetime opportunity! It's not every day you find a *T. rex*."

"Does it have a name?" Anna asked. "I've read that dinosaur fossils are often named after someone important."

"Well, this one is nicknamed Pete, nothing glamorous, I'm afraid. Peter was the name of the young undergraduate student who found the bones. Personally? I call it Pete's dragon, from the children's story!"

"I love it! Pete's dragon, also as in the dragon legends?" Anna asked, smiling.

"Yes, but don't let on to the others; they won't like it!

64

Well come on, my truck is over here. Why don't you follow me? The dig is not too far away, but it is an adventure to get to the dig itself," he ended cryptically. With that, he headed off to the ten-year old blue pickup truck.

"He seems nice enough," Christian commented, as he returned to the driver's seat he had so recently left.

"I wonder what he meant about an adventure?" Anna buckled her seat belt, pulling it snuggly across her chest.

"I guess we'll soon find out," Christian grinned.

They drove along the scenic road, which didn't have much traffic. There wasn't much of a draw this time of year without the fall leaves. In several weeks, when the leaves began to turn in earnest and in full autumn colors, there would be many tourists to enjoy the spectacular view.

"Great! More winding roads," Anna said. She grimaced at the proximity of the edge of the cliff to the drive.

"Come on, Anna, you've never complained like this before," Christian said, puzzled at his sister's attitude. Several years ago they had been on a family vacation to North Carolina. Both had tried mountain climbing and rappelling. She had no fear of heights then. She was usually the one jumping before she thought. This behavior was very unusual for her.

"I'm sorry, Christian. It's not your fault. I'm just not used to the sheer drops."

"No problem. You've got two weeks to get used to them." Christian smiled.

"Great." Anna frowned. Concentrating on a map of the park, she marked the map as they ventured ahead. They soon took a fork off the main road. Several turns later, they pulled up to a clearing with a travel trailer, several tents, and a campfire circle set off to one side. A few staff members worked at various tables under the trees. Pine needles padded the drive.

"Looks like we've arrived." Christian pulled up behind Luke's pickup. Rolling down the window, he asked, "Is there anyplace in particular you'd like me to park?"

"Sure, back by Rick's Jeep over there would be fine," Luke motioned to a camouflage Jeep next to a clump of trees with a small space beside them. "Rick's brother, Troy Lane, is the head of this excavation site."

Christian didn't mention he had already met Rick. He carefully parked the vehicle making sure not to scrape against any tree branches; it was a tight fit. "So, Rick is Troy's brother," Christian commented to Anna.

"Yeah, just as we suspected; they're related," Anna said.

Christian and Anna carefully exited from the tight space. Anna grabbed her backpack and jacket. She already felt colder due to the altitude.

"Is that all you brought?" Luke asked, eyeing Anna's lone jacket. "You know, for each 1,000 feet of increased elevation the temperature drops 3 to 5 degrees and that's not taking into consideration the wind-chill factor."

"We'll remember that next time," Anna assured him, zipping up her jacket.

"Yes, we were planning to take our main photos another time. Didn't Dr. Lane explain why we were coming today?" Christian asked.

"No. He doesn't tell me much. I'm on a need-to-know basis." Running a hand through his thin, blond hair, Luke sighed, "Sorry, kids, I shouldn't have said that."

"We were hoping to look at the dig today and find our way around the park. We plan to come back in a day or so to camp here and then spend several days at the dig," Anna smiled. "That way I can take some photos as the work progresses." She was excited to finally get a chance to do what she loved best.

"Several days, huh? I know I spoke with your Dad and the magazine, but things have changed a bit out here." He looked around to see if any of the staff were listening. Satisfied that no one could overhear, Luke continued. "Now Troy wants everything to go through him. Did Troy give you permission and a time you could stay?"

"No, he wanted to meet with us first. We were hoping to work around his schedule, but we're only going to be in Colorado for two weeks."

Luke hesitated, seeming to wrestle with what he was

going to say next. "I think you both should know that Troy is, well…difficult to get along with sometimes. He is especially unsympathetic to anyone who doesn't share his view of evolution. I know that your Dad has connections in high places, or this photo shoot wouldn't have had a chance to happen. Well, when Troy found out your Dad had been injured and was sending his kids instead, he almost blew a fuse." Luke couldn't help but smile at the memory.

"It was funny?" Anna asked.

"In a way," Luke explained. "You see Troy is an award-winning professor, and he plans to educate both of you in evolutionary teaching. He feels you must be misinformed."

"Oh." Christian and Anna exchanged glances. *Was Dr. Lane in for a surprise!*

"I don't mean to speak ill of Troy, but I'd like to warn you of what to expect. Even though I am not an evolutionist, at the university where I teach I must be very careful when explaining my personal views."

"You mean being politically correct?" Anna said.

"Yes, something like that," Luke agreed. "Let me show you around here quickly and then we'll descend to the dig. Follow me please," he muttered to himself, "This should be interesting."

Anna and Christian quickly followed Luke to the travel trailer. The door opened and they were surprised to find the interior had been turned into a working laboratory of sorts. The trailer's generator powered the electricity, and the room was larger than it had appeared at first glance. Inside, they found rows of neatly organized tools and supplies. Simon, a member of the staff, was busy cataloging some data. Luke introduced him to the Murphys.

"Troy sleeps in here," he motioned to a room in the back. "Over here we process and prepare the specimens we find," Luke explained. On two tables were stacks of cartons, several high-powered microscopes, and tools. "We take loose rocks and sediment and sift through making sure nothing has been overlooked. If we find something worth saving, we store the materials in these," Luke pointed to the clear plastic bags and cartons. "We then label them. The larger bones will be specially prepared, then transported by truck, or airlifted directly to the university. The better the job we do here, the easier it will be for those who will be reassembling the skeleton later."

Christian knew that sorting was the tedious side of any dig. Still, he was fascinated. "Do you keep a daily log about what you've found?"

"Yes, both Troy and I keep our own logs. We've basically split up the dig into two parts. He is in charge of the excavation, and I work on preparing the specimens and sorting to make sure nothing is overlooked." Luke smiled, "Definitely not glamorous."

"No sir," Christian added, "but necessary."

"I'm caught up on the preparation and will be working with the excavation for a while, so I'll come down with you. Are you interested in paleontology?"

"I'm interested in anything to do with ancient finds. More in the area of archaeology, but this is fascinating too. Do you think I might be able to help you?" Christian responded, his face glowing. "Anna won't need my help all the time."

"Sure, we can check with Troy. In fact we are preparing to lift one of the large leg bones today. That may be off limits, but I don't see why you can't help with the excavation." Luke patted Christian on the back. "Let's go to the dig."

Simon joined them as they walked to the edge of a precipice on Diamond Peak and looked at the valley below. He would help them in their descent.

"So, where is the dig?" Anna asked, puzzled.

"Two hundred feet down there," Luke pointed over the edge. Leaning down to pick up some gear. He tossed a harness to Christian. "The quickest way to get down is by rappelling. You have rappelled before, haven't you?"

Anna froze. He couldn't possibly be talking to her!

Chapter 9
The Adventure Begins

One look at Anna's face said it all. Luke looked surprised. "No one told you we would be rappelling?" Before she could answer he continued, "There is another path to the dig, but it takes about forty-five minutes and this way is much quicker."

"All I knew was that it was difficult to get to the dig, not that we had to rappel to get there. Right?" Anna asked Christian.

"Well . . .I did tell you that the people who found the bones were rappelling," Christian said. "I meant to tell you at breakfast this morning, that we would be rappelling too. You hadn't read Dad's report and his comments about the dig, and we were interrupted before I had a chance to tell you." Christian quickly told Luke about the paraglider that had crash-landed on their deck that morning.

"I should have read the report," Anna said and then shrugged. "I'm just surprised. Well, it will definitely be an adventure getting to the site. How far down did you say it was?"

"Two hundred feet," Luke said. Then remembering that

his first question was never answered, he asked it again; "You both rappel don't you?"

Christian saw that Luke looked concerned, so he put his mind at ease. "Yes, Anna and I have both rappelled before."

"Good, good," Luke said in relief.

"I did have fun the first time we tried rappelling," Anna smiled, both nervous and excited. Christian had caught on a bit more quickly to the daring sport than she had.

"Well, ándale, or whatever they say on TV," Anna said grinning.

The men began laughing, and Christian chuckled as he clued his sister in, "It's *on belay*, not *ándale!*"

Luke informed her. "Andale is Spanish for let's go, on *belay* on the other hand means to secure or make fast."

Anna laughed good naturedly at her mistake, "Okay, on belay."

Christian put on his climbing harness and adjusted the belt while Simon, who had been standing quietly listening to the exchange, helped Anna into her harness. She quickly remembered how to adjust it, tightening the leg loops and belt. After Luke had checked both harnesses, he asked Simon to radio below that they were coming. The young man did as he was asked and then walked over to a relatively large generator sitting to one side.

"This generator has a safety feature. It lets the backup safety line out gradually and doesn't allow you to drop too fast. I radioed Carlos and he will be the bottom belay." Simon pointed over the edge.

Luke gave a brief overview on rappelling. "Remember to try and stay in a sitting position while you push off with your feet. Keep your knees bent and don't push out too far. The safety rope won't let you go that fast. If you happen to lose your footing, stop the rope from sliding through your hand. Carlos will help from below. Keep your hand away from the figure eight and carabiner. Remember, descend slowly, and keep your right arm slightly bent as you let the rope run through your gloved hand. Don't try to stop it unless you have trouble."

"May I go down first?" Anna asked as much to get it over with as to see the dig. Luke looked a little surprised, but Christian smiled. His sister's yearn for adventure had returned.

Luke quickly agreed and started rummaging through the crate of equipment. He pulled out two leather gloves. "See if these fit," Luke tossed them both one glove. It took several tries to finally find a glove that fit them snugly. Luke helped Anna attach the carabiner, a peanut-shaped metal fastener, to her harness and then the figure eight onto the carabiner. An eight-millimeter rope ran through the figure eight.

Anna took a deep breath to brace herself. The hardest part about rappelling was heading over the side. The roar of the generator could be heard. Simon unclipped his two-way radio to tell Carlos, who was on the ledge, to hold the end of the rope already in place. Simon nodded okay, and Anna slowly walked backward over the edge.

It was bad enough to walk over the edge of a cliff, but backward? Anna leaned back, testing the rope as she went down. The sloping side soon became too steep to walk so Anna started pushing off with her legs. The safety rope held fast to the back of her harness, while the other rope passed through the figure eight and her right-gloved hand. The rope easily slid through her hand that was extended away from her body almost at a right angle. She could feel the slight heat in the rope as it sped through her hand. Anna now relived the exhilaration of feeling almost weightless as she dangled on a rope against the side of a mountain!

As Anna's feet neared the bottom of the ledge, she felt firm hands on her back helping her to land. Carlos was there as Luke had promised, immediately assisting her in removing the safety line and unhooking the rappel line. He tugged the safety line several times, signaling Luke to pull it up while the other rope remained stationary. Christian and Luke both slid down in record time, making it look easy.

Anna looked around as she waited for the others and was astounded by what she saw. The semicircular ledge on which she stood was about fifty feet wide and fifty feet deep. The cove-shaped ledge jutted out of the granite downwards-sloping mountainside. She turned toward the steady chipping going on by one of the five-man crew, who was painstakingly excavating a fossilized bone. An older man began walking toward her.

"That's awesome!" Anna gasped to no one in particular.

"Yes, it is," the bespectacled, stocky man said, extending his hand. "You must be Anna. I'm Dr. Lane."

Anna shook his firm grasp, trying not to stare up at his bald head. The sunlight glinting off the top made it hard. As if reading her thoughts, the stocky man removed a safari hat from his back pocket. "The sun is bright, and it will warm up nicely today. Did you know that September is the sunniest month here in the Rocky Mountains?"

Christian and Luke soon joined her. "No, I didn't know that."

"Many tourists miss out on the wonders of the park in September. Fortunately, you didn't have to fight the crowds that fall brings." Dr. Lane adjusted his wire-rimmed glasses. He shook Christian's hand. By way of introduction, he launched into a brief description of the dig.

"First, I'd like to warn you that this is an unprotected ledge. We are actually on a side segment of Diamond Peak. This is a diamond-shaped wall, which was etched out by glaciers many millions of years ago. It is considered the most spectacular alpine wall in the United States. The elevation at the peak is 14,000 feet, and we are a little more than half of the way up. So, here's a word of advice. Stay away from the edge. Is that understood?"

Both Anna and Christian nodded, as they looked downward at the breathtaking view. Several imposing mountains were in the distance, yet all at lower elevations.

Nodding, Dr. Lane continued, "As you can see, we have uncovered about three fourths of the *Tyrannosaurus*. We believe it is a full-grown specimen, and . . ." he dramatically paused for emphasis, "we believe it is articulated!"

"Articulated?" Anna inquired.

"Fully intact," Christian translated,

"That's right," Dr. Lane confirmed. "So far, no bones are missing."

"That's remarkable." Anna's photographer's eye was sizing up the situation. The sheer size of the dinosaur's fossilized remains seemed to dwarf the man working on excavating one particular bone.

"Many *Tyrannosaurus* bones have been found in Colorado, even though the *Stegosaurus* is considered the State dinosaur. Yet, because this is a *T. rex*, the size of the bones, not to mention their unusual appearance and the nature of the articulation, we are quite excited about this find." Dr. Lane admitted.

"Are you using any specific procedure to excavate?" Christian asked.

"Yes. We are using a very exacting mapping technique to excavate the bones quickly and efficiently without any damage. We use butcher paper to trace the bones full scale. This allows us a map showing how each bone was found and where it lay in relation to the rest of the animal. This will be invaluable when we are reassembling the bones back at the university." Dr. Lane paused to peer over his spectacles at the two to see if they were paying attention before he continued.

Luke interjected, "We also include leaves, invertebrates, and any micro-vertebrates found in the area. This has been very useful in the past when trying to put together a picture of the environment at the time. We map, collect, and label every bone as it is slowly uncovered. You should be able to get some great shots."

"Yes, well the mapping technique is my specialty. Besides speaking of pictures, we have been photographing our progress right along, which is why I wasn't sure we needed more photos. I expect you to stay out of the way and not interrupt any of the progress being made. Understood?" Dr. Lane asked.

"Oh yes, I understand. I prefer natural candid shots to reenactments whenever possible," Anna assured Dr. Lane.

Dr. Lane nodded his agreement before he continued. "We will soon apply generous plaster caps to the exposed bones. We are in the process of removing a portion of the overburden, the rock outcropping over the top of the bones." Dr. Lane pointed over his shoulder. "We cover the exposed areas each night with tarp, but the weathering process has begun, and it's very hard on them."

"We have a majority of the rock removed, so we believe we could get this done in a couple more weeks if the weather holds out," Luke added.

"We don't really know how long it will take to complete," Dr. Lane contradicted, glaring at Luke. "Each dig varies, and our major concern at this point is completing the excavation before the winter weather makes the excavation too dangerous. I would work around the clock if I could get the manpower. Yet, these men," he waved to the team working on the preparation of an extremely large leg bone, "treat this as a job. By 5:00 pm they expect to leave."

"Some of the men have families, as I do," Luke explained.

"My work is my family," Dr. Lane stated flatly.

Both Christian and Anna were uncomfortable by the veiled criticisms in the exchange and were hoping to get closer, but waited for Dr. Lane to invite them. The invitation came sooner than expected. "Won't you come this way?"

"I'll leave you to Troy's capable hands," Luke said, summarily dismissed by being ignored. Dr. Lane didn't answer, and the Murphys waved to Luke as they followed Dr. Lane. They didn't want to miss a closer look.

They would comment on Dr. Lane's rudeness toward Luke later. For now, Anna pulled her camera out of her backpack, hoping to take a couple of shots. She wordlessly handed the backpack to Christian, whose long strides outdistanced hers. Anna lagged a bit behind to take a shot from a distance. Moving back to the edge would provide a better shot, but she knew better than to make the attempt. After all they had been warned, and 7,000 feet was a long way down. She made a mental note to bring her wide-angle lens. After snapping a few shots, Anna slid the camera over her head and around her neck as she followed. She was just in time to hear Christian's question.

"Do you have any idea of the dimensions of this creature once it's completely excavated?"

"We know from other finds in North America that the *Tyrannosaurus rex* was about forty feet long and weighed as much as eight tons. We believe this creature will surpass that size. From the dimensions of the head alone, we believe it is five percent larger than any other fossil found to date."

"Wow, what was there?" Anna asked pointing to the gaping hole in the side of the mountain.

"The leg bone the men are currently readying to transport up was excavated from that area. I had a section of the overburden removed to keep the bone intact. It was the first bone found by some of our students earlier in the summer. The weathering has taken its toll, and it's cracked, so we decided to remove it before any further damage was done. Cracked bones are a way of life in paleontology, and it can be repaired," Dr. Lane scowled.

Anna looked at Christian and raised her eyebrows. *What was causing Dr. Lane to become angry? Was this the bone that Luke had mentioned earlier? If Dr. Lane was use to cracked bones, the leg bone cracking shouldn't have upset him. Or should it? Was he leaving out some information purposely?*

Christian wanted to shrug his shoulders, as if reading his sister's thoughts, but knew the gesture would be interpreted. Instead he asked, "How are you transporting the bone up the mountain?"

The question seemed to distract Dr. Lane from his musing, "We are hoping it won't be necessary to use a helicopter, and that most of the transportation can be made with the harness and generator. We are trying this today. As I said, Luke along with my brother, Rick are readying the bone to be transported. Before bones can be transported, we prepare the bones with a special adhesive such as PVA; that is Polyvinyl Acetate Beads, which we mix with acetone. This is a great, high-quality preservative coating. After this coating is applied we pack the bones in plaster. We also try to leave as much of the surrounding rock as possible."

"Doesn't that added weight increase the potential for damage given the size?" Christian asked, remembering the difficulty they had in the past with fossilized remains encased in plaster.

"Yes, but we have no choice in some instances where we cannot remove the bones without damaging them. We have more control in a lab than onsite. We have hired a pilot to airlift them out when needed."

"Do you mind if I get some shots of you with the fossil? If you stand over here," Anna pointed to the skull, "I won't get the others."

"If you insist." Dr. Lane gave a wry smile and stood before the partially exposed skeleton of the head. "How about this?" he asked.

"That's great, hold it," Anna said as she expertly took several shots in succession.

"Okay, now could you hold some sort of tool, a pick perhaps?"

"Like this?" Dr. Lane lifted a pick from a small nearby table and held it on the rock as if he were chipping away the hardened sandstone.

"Yes, that's perfect." Anna smiled. *So much for having a difficult time, Dr. Lane was cooperating beautifully. Perhaps we will be done with the pictures much sooner than I planned.* "That was wonderful," she said aloud.

"How about a shot with Luke and the leg bone? Would you like a picture with him?" Christian offered.

"Not necessarily." The firmness in his tone brooked no argument.

"Okay," Anna said cheerfully; "I guess that's all."

"Well now, that was easy," Dr. Lane brightened. "That was much quicker than I expected. You are quite the professional young lady. I hope you have a nice trip back to Florida."

Anna was able to stifle a laugh before it gave them away, while Christian held his expression to tightly controlled amusement. Apparently Dr. Lane thought the entire photo shoot was over. Anna and Christian exchanged glances. Who would break the news to him that they wanted to come back several more times?

"Um, Dr. Lane," Anna ventured, "We'd like to come back if we could and take more pictures."

76

"More? I thought you were done." Dr. Lane looked annoyed to find that he was not rid of them yet.

"Well there is a certain procedure my Dad wants me to use. I'm to take photos at different times of the day and in a certain order. I also will be using various lenses and filters. Each of these gives..."

"Yes, yes," Dr. Lane waved his hand impatiently not interested in the details of photography, "I see." He hesitated while apparently thinking. "How long do you think you will need?"

"I could be done in two or three days. Would it be possible to camp here while we are working on this?"

Thunder rumbled overhead. Dr. Lane glanced at the sky, ignoring the question. "There's your answer. You need to get up top now. The weather here is highly unpredictable, but one thing is for certain, thunderstorms crop up quickly and one is certainly brewing now."

Anna looked above in dismay. The sky had been clear, except for a few cumulous clouds. Now those same clouds looked dark and foreboding. "I've read that storms crop up often in the summer," Christian added, "but it's the beginning of fall."

"Well, tell that to the sky," Dr. Lane grimaced. "In the mountains you respect 'Mother nature'. The rule is to be at tree line in a storm. If not, and you are the highest object around don't expect to live to tell about it."

"Should we call you about a schedule that will work for you?" Anna stubbornly refused to leave without an answer.

Christian set down the backpack he was holding, for he knew that this could take a while. He folded his arms as he listened to their exchange.

"Dr. Lane! Could you come here, we need your help immediately!" Carlos, one of the staff yelled. The dinosaur leg bone was suspended midway up the mountain on a harness. Several men were shouting from above and the crew below was holding the ropes taut.

"How about Thursday?" Dr. Lane dismissed them as he hurried toward the group of men raising the dinosaur leg bone.

"Isn't he going to get out of the rain?" Anna lowered her

voice as she asked Christian; yet saw the opportunity of another great shot.

"I don't know, but we don't have much time to get up and remain dry," Christian said. He picked up the backpack, as the rumbling of thunder grew louder.

Anna aimed her camera at the group slowly working to raise the heavy leg bone up the mountainside. Several shots later she lowered her camera. "I think they are having trouble raising the bone."

Before Christian could comment a loud bellow was heard. Shouts came from several of the men warning them to run as they scattered out of the way. Anna and Christian tried to run to safety as they watched in stunned astonishment. The mammoth dinosaur leg bone had slipped off the harness and was plummeting straight toward them!

Chapter 10
Fossilized Bones?

The bone came crashing down the mountainside. Loosened pebbles rained down in its wake. Anna and Christian managed to run to a tiny shelter where the other men were cowering. The bone careened as it slid and a deafening thud was heard, as the bone forcefully hit the ledge and cracked in two. It continued to slide and came to a rest a few feet away from the stunned crew.

No one appeared to move for several moments before mayhem erupted. Rick yelled at Luke, Troy thundered orders to Carlos, and the other two crewmembers ran, picking up supplies scattered by the fallen leg bone. No one, it seemed, wanted to be the first to mention the obvious. The wonderfully preserved bone was now lying on the ground, broken into two pieces.

Anna and Christian thought it best to stay as far out of the way as possible. They stood under a small rock outcropping. Rain still looked imminent, but now was not a good time to request help from Luke to climb up. If they knew the way, the path would be the passage of choice.

"Of course it can be fixed!" Dr. Lane thundered in answer to Rick's statement that repairs could easily be made, "But should we have to fix it? That is the question!" Dr. Lane fumed at Luke, "Weren't you overseeing this?"

"Yes, but the specimen appears to have caught on a jagged ledge. The bone wedged itself up under a small outcropping. When Simon tried to pull it up with the generator, the rope tension pulled the harness, but the bone tilted and then, well..." Luke trailed off not wanting to restate the obvious.

Dr. Lane took note of Anna and Christian for the first time, surprised to see them still there. His eyes narrowed when he saw the camera in Anna's hand, "Why haven't you two left yet?"

"We didn't have a chance sir—the bone— " Christian quickly rushed to add, "We'll just take the path," pointing in the general direction.

"I'll show you the way," Luke volunteered, as much to be helpful as to escape further interrogation from Dr. Lane. He hurried over, showing them the path with quick directions about reaching the top. He ended with a promise to join them later.

An hour later a drenched Christian and Anna reached the parking area at the top. Although they had walked up the steep incline as quickly as they could, they were still hindered by the rainstorm. They were thankful once again to the Sullivans and the nice quality of jackets, which had protected their clothing, for the most part from getting wet. They arrived just in time to watch the second piece of bone being brought up to the top. Dr. Lane had remained below, with Rick, and was already working on another section of bone to be excavated.

Luke and the remaining crew had climbed up. The others were calling it a day while Luke was assessing the damage.

The only one who camped at the dig was Dr. Lane and occasionally Simon or Carlos. Rick, and Luke, along with several others lived in the nearby town.

He shook his head, wiping the moisture off his brow, "This really isn't that bad we can fix it," he smiled at Anna and Christian. "In paleontology, broken bones are the norm but when a bone is found with just a few hairline cracks, and then it's broken while transporting ... well, that is disappointing."

Christian knelt beside the massive bone, studying the fractured center. Taking care not to touch anything, He pointed curiously. "What's this, Luke? Does the bone always appear so splintered, or is this due to the break?" Christian pointed to a section near the center of the bone that looked less stone-like than the outer portion of the fossilized bone.

"Yes, I see what you mean." Luke peered closely at the section of bone, taking out a pocketknife and carefully inserting an edge into the center. "Hmm, that's odd. It looks like, well, it looks almost..." Luke looked startled at what he was about to say.

Lifting his head he looked to see who was nearby, "Hey Simon, come here."

Christian wanted to ask a hundred questions, but he carefully chose one, "Do you think we could take a fragment and magnify it? I noticed you have a microscope set up in the trailer."

"Yes, that's a good idea," Luke sent Simon to retrieve a petri dish, sharp pick, and other materials he needed.

Meanwhile, Anna, thankful that the rain had ceased, used the opportunity to take pictures. She hadn't brought any special lenses for taking close-ups so she made do with what she had. She waited until Luke was busy before nudging her brother.

"What's going on? What do you see?" The center of the bone looked like a fossil to her.

"I'm not sure. Something is not right. I don't know what we'll see, but since Luke has a microscope in the trailer we can take a closer look." Christian replied.

Glancing at her watch Anna said, "Don't you think we should get back for dinner?"

"No, especially if it means formal dress." Christian grinned holding out his cell phone to Anna, "How about calling the Sullivans and telling them we've been held up here. We can stop for something to eat on the way home."

"Good idea," Anna grinned, taking the phone. "I'll let you know what they say." Anna walked over to the Hummer to make the call. Several minutes later she walked back to see the men kneeling around the bone taking samples of the material to view. Christian caught her eye and she nodded her head that yes, the delay was not a problem.

"Well, let's see what we have." Luke said, taking the container with fragments into the trailer. Anna and Christian were close behind, while Simon worked on covering the exposed, cracked, fossilized bone with resin.

The lights in the trailer were not nearly as bright as in a real lab, yet they would have to do. Luke carefully took a sharp knife and cut a thin sliver off of one of the fragments to look at under the microscope. "I've never run across this before. This is really interesting, the way this section of the fossil seems ... to be..." Luke muttered to himself. Christian and Anna hung on every word and tried to decipher his meaning.

Luke adjusted the knobs and then refocused them again as he peered into the eyepiece. He looked surprised but didn't say a word as he prepared another piece of the specimen to view under the microscope.

"May I take a look?" Christian asked, not wanting to appear rude yet dying to see what Luke had observed.

"Sure," Luke said in an offhanded manner, not lifting his head as he worked to prepare the next specimen.

Christian squinted one eye and looked into the eyepiece, "Whoa, is that what I think it is?" Christian looked up, smiling.

"What do you think it is?" Luke asked as he licked his lower lip.

Anna watched the exchange, noting Luke's uneasiness and Christian's excitement, "What? What did you see?" She peered into the eyepiece seeing what appeared to be a segment of bone.

"It looks like...bone that is not fully fossilized." Christian said matter-of-factly.

Unknowingly, Luke had been holding his breath. Now he let out a big sigh, "Yep, that's exactly what I saw. And, that is either great news or horrible news, depending on which side of the fence you stand."

82

"Why?" Anna said, still unsure of what the fuss was about. Slowly she looked from Christian to Luke, "Wait a minute, if the bone is fossilized it means it has basically turned to rock ... okay, I know that's not the exact term but ... after millions of years, according to evolutionists, there shouldn't be any unfossilized bone left, right?"

"You guessed it, you win the grand prize!" Luke said, sitting down elated. He had just looked at the second slide; pointing to the microscope he invited Christian to take a look, "That shows the same thing."

"What are you going to do?" Christian said, his face showing his delight. "This is wonderful. It is just what Creationists believe! The world is not old. Finding a dinosaur bone that is fresh enough to see under a microscope proves it!"

"Hold on!" Luke held up his hands in protest, "We know the world is not millions of years old, but this doesn't prove anything. We need to take this one step at a time. There are many tests we can run on a portion of the bone back at the university lab in order to either verify or disprove this finding."

"Great. A university that teaches evolution as fact is going to back you up. Fat chance." Christian said in disgust.

"One thing I will say, the lab technicians are very professional when it comes to this kind of thing. They will report the results but perhaps have a different interpretation as to why there appears to be unfossilized bone here." Luke said, standing and carefully removing the specimens to get them ready to transport to the lab.

"Christian didn't mean they would purposefully be dishonest." Anna said, glaring at her brother.

"Well," Christian grinned sheepishly, "I guess I'm just used to having the cards stacked against us whenever the topic is brought up. I've read of many labs changing results to fit a scientist's given hypothesis."

"Yes, so have I," Luke sighed, "Let's hope in this case the truth prevails. What I'm really dreading is telling Troy about this."

Both Christian and Anna were glad neither of them had

that responsibility, as they gathered their things to leave. They wanted to be as far away as possible when Dr. Troy Lane found out there was the possibility of unfossilized bone being found in his precious *Tyrannosaurus rex*!

Chapter 11
Animal Skins

The next morning back at the Sullivans' home, Anna and Christian once again ate a solitary breakfast on the deck. The weather was a bit cooler than the day before, yet they couldn't imagine eating indoors when given the choice. They had taken a tour of the house that morning, courtesy of Cindy who was a tall, thin, fidgety lady. The blonde-haired woman had been directed by the Sullivans to make sure Anna and Christian knew their way around. Christian had been particularly impressed with the expansive library. The floor-to-ceiling bookshelves lined three walls. A spectacular view of the lake could be seen from the fourth floor, with an inviting padded window seat along the edge. The library even included a moveable ladder that could reach the second story shelves.

"So, what are we going to do today?" Anna asked, reaching for the salt. Before Christian could respond, the Sullivans waltzed up.

"There you are! I almost didn't believe Hilary and Cindy

when they said you were on the deck." Mrs. Sullivan threw up her hands in disbelief. "And there you are."

"How did you like Cindy?" Mrs. Sullivan asked.

"She was very nice." Anna was surprised by the question because Mrs. Sullivan seemed to just tolerate the hired help.

"Cindy, and Sam manage the home most of the time, but occasionally fill in so the others can have time off. I really like her," Mrs. Sullivan said, pulling up a chair.

"Is it always so cold here?" Anna asked, shivering at the slight breeze off the lake.

"Most of the time, but tis a fine day to be outdoors! Go on with you, now." Mr. Sullivan said.

Sometimes Mr. Sullivan's Irish phrases were a puzzle to Anna, so she just smiled politely.

"So, what have you planned?" Mr. Sullivan joined those seated.

"Actually we were talking about it earlier," Christian said. "Scott Song Le, the next-door neighbor, called and invited us to his house this morning. He wanted us to meet his parents. Later, we're to meet them in town to have lunch with Scott and his sister."

"Can't say I know the boy or his family," Mr. Sullivan said.

"His father was on the Song Glider that we watched the other evening," Anna said. She quickly informed the Sullivans about how they had met Scott.

"What an interesting family." Mr. Sullivan chuckled. "We'll meet the neighbors after we've settled in a bit and have more time. If you don't mind... perhaps for the time being ... not inviting guests over."

"We wouldn't think of imposing on your hospitality." Anna exclaimed.

"Oh, it's not that, my goodness." Mrs. Sullivan huddled in her oversized, peach cashmere, sweater with matching leggings. "We haven't had a second to slow down, and we want to spend some time with you two this morning."

"Sure," Anna said, happy for the opportunity. Perhaps

the Sullivans would tell them some stories about times spent with their grandparents.

"We'd love to hear about the days when you lived near our grandparents," Christian said, as if reading Anna's thoughts.

"Oh, we don't want to bore you young people with old stories," Mr. Sullivan replied.

"We have plenty of time to reminisce later," Mrs. Sullivan said. "Now I'd love to show what I bought for you yesterday, Anna. Come inside and see."

"We loved the clothes you've already given us," Anna said, referring to the sweaters and jackets they had found in their rooms the previous morning. "That was so sweet of you! Please don't feel like you need to buy us anything else."

"Wait until you see what she bought," Mr. Sullivan chuckled, smiling at Christian and, in an aside, said, "Stay out here laddie, and she'll come back here to show you."

Anna glanced back at Christian, with an uneasy feeling in the pit of her stomach, as she followed Mrs. Sullivan. The wood floors echoed her staccato heels as Mrs. Sullivan made her way past the white leather couch. On the glass-topped, marble, coffee table stood a stack with boxes and bags, all sporting names of designer clothing. A small-wheeled metal rack stood beside the table with padded hangers and zippered bags.

"Let's start with the biggie!" Mrs. Sullivan cooed, as she unzipped a black bag with flourish. "Well, isn't it lovely?"

"It will look wonderful on you," Anna warmly acknowledged, as Mrs. Sullivan held up the camel-colored, knee-length fur coat.

"Oh, but you are a darling. This is not for me; it's for you!"

Anna stood speechless as Mrs. Sullivan proceeded to drape the mink over her shoulders, encouraging her to try the coat on. Her mother had told her of the Sullivans' generosity to the family in the past, but this was totally unbelievable.

"Oh, I couldn't!" Anna insisted, cheeks flaming at the thought of wearing a coat of this value, much less a fur.

"I'll not hear of it," Mrs. Sullivan insisted. "Come over

here to the mirror and have a look."

Anna slowly walked over. If there had been an escape, she would have used it in a heartbeat. She looked at herself in the mink and almost laughed out loud. Her eyes began to sparkle, and a small giggle escaped. She placed her chin-length hair behind her ears in a nervous gesture and shuffled her Nikes as she stood under Mrs. Sullivan's scrutiny. Anna looked like a kid in her mother's coat.

"Hmm, I see what you mean." Mrs. Sullivan agreed she appeared to be thinking the same thing. "It is a wee bit big, and the sneakers don't quite go with the coat," she laughed. "But the color is lovely on you," she said as she adjusted the collar up higher around Anna's neck. "Now go on, and show your brother and Johnson. They'll adore it."

Anna wanted to run up to her room and lock the door. She'd never live this down, never. She could just imagine what Christian would say. Anna followed Mrs. Sullivan outdoors, wishing she could blend into the woodwork. Shoulders slumping in the oversized fur, Anna stuffed her hands into the pockets and shuffled her feet.

Christian took the last sip of his orange juice and began choking as Anna walked onto the deck. His eyes watered as much from choking as from laughter. He quickly held the linen napkin up to his mouth.

"My goodness, how lovely you look!" Mr. Sullivan said, unaffected by Christian. "You do have an eye for style, Sarah," he beamed at his wife, as he held out a chair so that she could join him.

"I told Mrs. Sullivan I just couldn't accept such a generous gift, right Christian?" Anna insisted and her eyes pleaded with her brother to agree. She wanted to stomp her foot in frustration. *This isn't funny* she inwardly fumed.

"Well, maybe you could phone Mom and Dad and ask them?" Christian suggested, recovering from his choking spell. His eyes were still glistening, but there was no disguising his enjoyment of Anna's predicament.

"What a splendid idea," Mrs. Sullivan said.

"No!" Anna almost shouted then she lowered her voice. "It's not that I don't appreciate your kindness. It's just that in Florida I'd never use such a wonderful coat…" She trailed off at a loss for words.

"You know, she's right," Christian said, coming to Anna's rescue with a wink. "Our winters rarely reach thirty degrees, with highs often in the seventies and eighties, so she would rarely be able to wear the coat. Besides, she'd have to keep the coat in storage or it would become ruined by insects." Christian remembered his grandfather complaining about having to periodically retrieve his grandmother's fur from storage.

Mrs. Sullivan laughed at the oversight. "My darling, a fur is fashionable in all weather. I insist that you keep it."

"Thanks," Anna said, defeated.

"Go on, see what else she bought," Mr. Sullivan urged.

"Not more clothing!" Anna said, horrified by the thought. "You've done so much already."

Just then Susan walked out to the deck with a small, gleaming, silver carafe and several china cups. "Here is your coffee, Mr. Sullivan." She eyed Anna and the fur but said nothing.

"Come, Anna," Mrs. Sullivan said, "Susan, I'll have my coffee in the living room. Anna would you like anything to drink?"

"No, thank you." Anna smiled at Susan, but the young girl averted her glance. Anna felt dismayed and wondered about how it must look to be sporting fur coats and ordering people around without even a please or thank you. There was nothing she could say now, so she silently followed Mrs. Sullivan. She just prayed there were no more big surprises.

Out on the deck, Mr. Sullivan lit a cigarette, hiding it from view. Christian couldn't help but look at Mr. Sullivan in surprise.

"I know this is a bad habit, and my wife doesn't approve, so I'm only allowed to smoke outdoors," he said, as way of explanation for his covert actions. "Go on, tell me about the excavation. What did you find?"

Christian filled him in on the *Tyrannosaurus* and the

difficulty in reaching the dig. He purposely left out the warning Luke had given about Dr. Lane's attitude.

"A *Tyrannosaurus*, my word. I might like to come take a look."

"We could ask for permission, sir. It is a long climb down, but you seem to be in good shape."

"Yes, I feel like I'm twenty years old," Mr. Sullivan chuckled. "You are as old as you feel, young man. You'll do well to remember that! Our minds never age, but our bodies do."

Christian smiled, somehow knowing that Mr. Sullivan truly believed he felt twenty years old. He didn't look twenty by any stretch of the imagination. His lined face and hands and gray hair, while stylishly combed, reflected every bit of his age.

"By the way, I loved the Hummer. What a vehicle!" Christian enthused.

They launched into a discussion about the all-terrain vehicle, which ensued for thirty minutes until Anna returned. Mrs. Sullivan was directing Susan to hang the clothing she had purchased for Anna and Christian in their closets. Anna couldn't wait to see Christian's face when he heard about the suit purchased for him by the Sullivans. If Anna had to wear wool and taffeta, it was only fair that Christian had to wear a suit.

Mr. Sullivan's cell phone rang. "Yes? Hold please." Pushing a button on the phone, eyes twinkling, he rose, taking Sarah's arm, and led her from the deck.

"We'll leave you two now, we're headed out." Mrs. Sullivan waved as she left the room. A trail of expensive perfume lingered.

"What was that all about?" Christian asked.

"Which part?" Anna rejoined. Within minutes, Susan came in with a portable phone, "It's for you."

Christian took the receiver and after listening for a minute smiled saying, "Hi Mom!"

"Oh great!" Anna said as she flounced onto the spring backed cushioned chair. Wait until her Mom heard about the fur coat.

Chapter 12
The Discovery

With a population of 6000, the small town of Eldorado Springs had an astonishing amount of designer clothing shops interspersed with rustic homegrown ones. The small town definitely sported character, cleverly nestled in a valley amid the breathtaking panorama of the Rocky Mountains. The local town was known for its world famous Eldorado Springs Resort, and perhaps more notably the distribution of its bottled spring water.

That afternoon, Scott, and his sister, Kayla, were going to show the Murphys around town. Kayla had a dentist appointment that morning and had permission to take the rest of the day off from school. The foursome met as planned at the park, which sported a small fountain and various play structures.

Kayla's waist-length, jet-black hair was worn loose; she looked petite and fragile next to her tall brother. The Murphys would soon find that looks could be deceiving.

"Kayla, I'd like to introduce you to the Murphys." Scott lost no time in pulling a pair of tennis shoes out of his backpack.

"Here, Christian, these are for you."

"Oh, please! What a great way to begin a friendship!" Kayla rolled her eyes. "Don't take them if you value your life."

Christian shrugged and took the high-top, black and white sneakers. He looked at them, puzzled. "Thanks, but I have shoes." He held up one foot to prove his point.

"Not like these babies; turn them over," Scott said proudly.

Christian did as he was told, and saw retractable wheels underneath, like those on in-line skates, "Awesome!" He quickly sat on the bench and began to unlace his shoes.

"We can skate around town and walk in the stores. There aren't any brakes, so you need to press down on your heel or toe to stop. These are heavy-duty, stainless steel, urethane wheels that roll great!"

"Anna and I are going to use the limo, so don't even think of giving us a pair," Kayla held up a hand in protest.

Anna was surprised to hear the news. Shopping with a chauffer? *Will I ever be able to return to my normal life?*

"No, I have something else for you two. I knew you wouldn't want to go shopping with us, so I thought we could keep in touch with these." Scott gave Anna a wristwatch with a small antenna protruding on one end.

"Can't we just use our cell phones?" Kayla asked more than a bit annoyed. "Do you two see what I have to live with?" she asked. She feigned exasperation, but she looked proud of her brother.

"I think it's great," Anna said laughingly as she strapped the oversized watch to her purse handle, "but doesn't this have a short range?"

"Actually, no. That's why it's a bit bigger than most watches. I've boosted the transmitters and it should have a four-mile range, which we can test," Scott said proudly. He quickly showed Anna how to use it.

"Notice he didn't give it to me to use," Kayla said. "Come on, Anna, daylight is burning, and we have shopping to do before lunch, which my poor mouth may protest," Kayla gingerly rubbed her jaw where a new filling had been placed that morning.

After agreeing to meet at 2:00pm for a late lunch at *Larkin's,* a favorite deli, the boys took off skating down the street. They were headed for an electronic store to pick up parts for another new invention.

Kayla meanwhile, took Anna shopping, after dropping off a small bag of film to be developed at a one-hour photo shop. Anna really didn't mind shopping for about an hour or so, but she soon found that shopping with Kayla was like being caught up in a whirlwind.

Meanwhile, Christian was surprised to discover that Scott was a favorite in every shop they entered. All the owners knew him by name. He walked in and out of three shops managing to obtain the exact part or piece he needed, and for half its original cost.

"It's not what you know, it's who you know," Scott said with a smile when Christian commented on everyone's friendliness.

Skating down the sidewalk, Scott said, "Did you see last night's episode of *101 Most Wanted?*"

"No, what happened?" Christian questioned with interest.

"These guys are now on the 101 most wanted list."

"What for?"

"Stealing inventions," Scott said with a grin. "Just kidding! The show went on to say they are thought to be around thirty years old and have eluded the police on countless occasions. Okay, here's the cool part," Scott paused, dragging out the story, before continuing. "They steal identities. According to the program, they steal social security numbers, and can really wreck a person's credit. The police have been calling them the 'I.D. Snatchers' and say they are very dangerous."

"How strange! Is that it?"

"Well, the program ended with vague descriptions of what they look like and, of course, a number to call if you've seen them. They said that the criminals have spent millions in a matter of days. You know, I bet Kayla could do that."

Christian laughed along with Scott. "That show sounds a bit far fetched; are there always stories like that on the program?"

"Yeah, they are usually pretty interesting ones, but sometimes they're especially strange."

"Hey, let's call the girls," Scott said, as he spoke into his walky-watch. Soon Anna replied and they briefly conversed. After saying good-bye, Scott figured the range was somewhere within the five-mile zone. Smiling, he said, "This is working better than I thought!"

The boys ended their conversation as they retracted their rollers and headed into another hardware store.

Once they were headed down the sidewalk again, Christian asked, "Is this for your dad's latest invention? I really enjoyed meeting him this morning." He smiled as he thought about Mr. Song Le. He was a hyper, older version of Scott. The basement of his large spacious home had been converted into a workshop. Christian could have stayed there for days looking at his gadgets.

"The part I just picked up is going into an invention of my own, not Dad's." Pride filled his voice as he continued, "I'm going to use the scientific principle of magnetic resonance. When my invention is strapped onto the fuel line of any vehicle, it will enable a car to burn half as much fuel as before. This is accomplished by spreading out the molecular make up of the gas. The best part is it will save money and reduce pollution!"

"The Hummer needs that! It's a gas guzzler." Christian added, "I bet anything to do with saving the environment is a big seller."

"You're right. It has advertising potential. I plan to strike it rich on this one, and then Dad won't be so bummed about . . ." Scott tailed off. He recovered quickly and changed the subject.

Christian didn't comment on Scott's unfinished sentence, but surmised that Scott and his father didn't always see eye to eye. He didn't know Scott well enough to ask any questions and he didn't want to pry.

*   *   *   *   *   *   *   *   *

94

Meanwhile, in another part of town, Kayla was dragging Anna into designer shop after designer shop with prices so high Anna had nearly choked when she first saw them.

"How does this look?" Kayla asked for what seemed like the billionth time and for the zillionth outfit.

Anna looked at the pretty girl in front of her. Her dark hair offset her slightly slanted eyes, which looked as if they were black liquid. Anna switched her attention to the outfit, "I like the front, but I'm not sure about the back . . ." Anna studied the outfit with a photographer's eye.

"Yeah, that's the part I'm not sure about too. How do you do it?" Kayla turned not waiting for an answer and headed into the dressing room again.

Kayla smiled as she changed outfits; she had taken to Anna right off for her 'unique style,' as she liked to put it. Kayla was pleased to learn that Anna had a knack for critiquing and picking out outfits. Anna didn't share that this talent was sharpened from her years of experience as a photographer.

Kayla exited the dressing room, wearing a stunning jade sweater atop a denim knee-length skirt. She stretched out her arms in a what-do-you-think gesture. Anna smiled. "It's perfect!"

As they were about to exit the store, the driver, who had been leaning against the limo, jumped up and ran to hold open the door to the store. He took the bags from Kayla's hands. Siding up to the limo, the driver opened the door for them and then deposited the huge shopping bags into the trunk. Kayla was ready to hop in, when Anna spotted a secondhand bookstore just down the street.

"Hey Kayla could we please go to that book store? I absolutely love old books."

Kayla was happy to see Anna so excited about shopping, even if it was a used bookstore.

The two girls walked arm and arm into the shop. Chimes sounded loudly to announce their presence as the door shut behind them. The dim lights and musty smell of books assailed their senses. Kayla prettily put her hand across her nose and mouth as she tried not to breathe.

"Good day, girls," came a soprano voice from the rear as a tall, wiry lady emerged, carrying a stack of books she couldn't see over.

Anna greeted the woman warmly, while Kayla stiffly ignored her.

Anna didn't seem to notice the musty odor as her eyes eagerly scanned the subject dividers on top of the shelves. Books of all shapes and sizes lined both walls and shelves from floor-to-ceiling and in between. Her eyes alighted on several tables set up in the middle of the store. She headed for them, with Kayla in tow. The small card table held a hand-printed sign that read, 'Books for $1.00.' Anna suddenly smiled at the irony of the situation. She had gone straight to the bargain table, while moments ago what Kayla had spent on one belt could buy one hundred books.

"Look at this," Anna held up a hardbound black book.

"Cool! Ancient legends. I've heard several scary ones," Kayla brightened.

Carefully flipping through the book, Anna came across several interesting stories none of which were scary. "These stories look like folklore."

Kayla shrugged her shoulders disinterestedly. "What happened to the scary legends?"

After much consideration, Anna selected a mystery novel and the ancient legends book. Upon flipping through the book, she found an account of a worldwide flood that caught her attention. *Hmmm ... interesting ... a flood,* Anna thought. *Wonder if it has anything to do with the flood mentioned in the book of Genesis?*

Anna was about to head for the register, when Kayla jumped, grabbing her arm. The sound of the clanging chimes on the door announced the arrival of another customer. Kayla recovered quickly as she watched a nondescript man of medium height and weight with brown hair and eyes walk into the store. His attire, however, was one that couldn't be missed; he came in wearing a parka-style coat, with a camera hanging around his neck and a large road map dangling from his left hand.

Seeing Anna and Kayla staring at him, he waved and with a side smile said, "Hi girls. How are you doing? My name is Willy Burns."

"Ah, hi," Anna answered, trying to hide a smile. She had been cold upon arriving in Colorado, but if she was cold, then he must be freezing. Even she didn't think the weather warranted wearing a parka!

"I've come to see the sights. I'm a tourist, as if you couldn't tell," he chuckled, and unashamedly holding up his tour book and map with pleasure. "Are you two from around here?"

Kayla turned away to stifle a laugh as she shuffled through a pile of books on the table behind. "We need to go, Anna," Kayla urged, with her back toward the man.

Anna smiled. "I'm not from around here either, but my friend has been living here for a while." Anna motioned to Kayla.

"Well, I think you young ladies may be able to help me . . ."

"You'd have to see a doctor for that kind of help," Kayla mumbled, but only Anna heard her.

The man continued, "I've come in looking for the nearest post office. I've got to mail Mom a postcard."

Kayla quickly gave the verbal directions he requested.

"Okay, thanks." He walked to the exit, and the jangling caused both girls to turn and look up at the door. Before either girl could protest, the man lifted his camera and snapped their picture.

Chapter 13
Ancient Legends?

"Hope you don't mind," he said good-naturedly once he had already taken the picture. Anna and Kayla stood shocked as they watched the man practically run out the door.

"That was strange!" Anna asked Kayla, "Do people act like that all the time?"

"No, that's a first. Why would he want to take our picture? I don't like it." Kayla murmured as they walked to the sales counter.

The sales clerk wiped her hands on a napkin before accepting the books from Anna. "Oh, excuse me. I try to eat whenever there's a free second," she apologized.

"Lunch!" Anna gasped in horror, glancing down at her watch. "We're supposed to meet Scott and Christian at the Cafe in five minutes!"

"Oh, well. Scott knows me. I'm *always* fashionably late," Kayla said dismissively, but she seemed concerned and continued to look over her shoulder.

Anna didn't comment. She disliked being late and never

thought it was fashionable. Once Anna paid for the books, both girls headed out the store and climbed into the limo.

Anna sighed in relief as they pulled up to the Cafe. A quick glance at her watch revealed that they were only a few minutes late.

"Hey, Christian, Scott, sorry we're late," Anna apologized as the two girls approached. The boys had already chosen a table and ordered soft drinks.

"Actually, you're early by Kayla's standards," Scott teased. "Kayla should take you shopping more often."

"Hello, Christian," Kayla said with a smile. She then sat stiffly ignoring Scott as she picked up the menu, pretending he wasn't even there.

Scott shrugged at his sister's rudeness. "So, did you buy out the stores?"

"Yes, on your expense account," Kayla replied sarcastically.

Anna and Christian exchanged puzzled looks as they watched the exchange. They had already noticed that Kayla and Scott did not have the same easygoing relationship that they did.

Once the foursome was served, a beeping sound was heard. Scott immediately grabbed what looked like a pocket calculator. "I've got mail!" Scott laughed, hitting a button to acknowledge receipt of the e-mail. "I'm sure it's nothing that can't wait until later."

"Awesome!" Christian asked, "You can read your e-mail on that?"

"Yes, it's really quite simple..." Scott began to explain, showing Christian his hand-held device.

"Hold it you two, before you get side-tracked," Anna interrupted. "Something odd happened to us a bit earlier."

Both boys immediately wanted details. Anna quickly told them about the strange man, while Kayla added comments here and there. "He got the directions, snapped our picture, and left. I have never seen anyone act that weird!"

"I don't like the idea of a total stranger taking your pictures," Scott said, with a frown as he chewed on his sandwich.

"This comes from a guy who walks around with gadgets in his pocket?" remarked Kayla. "What are you afraid of? That we're going to be kidnapped and held for ransom?" Kayla was only half serious as she nervously toyed with her piping hot soup.

"Maybe," Scott responded. Sighing he informed the Murphys, "Over the years, Dad has received various threats. That's one of the reasons Kayla is not allowed to go out alone and why Dad sends the chauffeur."

"He looked harmless," Anna offered. "He had kind eyes."

"What? Like a puppy?" Scott teased. The others started to laugh.

The lunch conversation then turned to small talk about their purchases. After hearing the long list of items Kayla had bought, Christian said, "Anna, I sure hope you didn't spend your life's savings as well."

"No, Christian," Anna said with a laugh. "I only bought two books. I found a really interesting book on ancient legends."

"Really? Let's see."

Anna opened her bag, retrieved the book, and handed it to her brother.

Meanwhile Scott reached over and took half of his sister's uneaten sandwich. "You don't want that do you?" he gestured. Seeing her shake her head, he hungrily wolfed down a part of the sandwich. He turned to his friend and mumbled, "You're really into ancient studies, aren't you, Christian? "

"I guess I am. I like studying the way ancient cultures lived, the puzzle of trying to piece together ancient artifacts, and coming up with a relative chronology."

"Huh?" Kayla asked, "English, please. What's a relative chronology."

"Well, it's a way that archeologists estimate a time frame in dating their finds. In other words it tells them a little about when the artifact possibly was used and by whom. Unfortunately circular reasoning is often used."

"Which means?" Kayla asked.

"Artifacts, or for that matter bones, are often age-dated at the time when scientists theorize the layers were laid down,"

Christian explained. "They say a fossil is x-number of years old because it was found in rock strata thought to be that old."

"Then," Anna continued, "the scientists age-date the rocks or layers in the earth's strata by the fossil or artifact that is found."

"You're kidding, right?" Kayla said.

"We are simplifying it a bit. They use what they call an 'index' fossil."

"Which is?" Kayla asked.

"It's a particular type of fossil that has only been found in a certain type of rock strata, in more than one location. Scientists have interpreted this as meaning the animal must have lived only in that particular time. They figured out a way to date the age of the surrounding rock accordingly."

"So, what's wrong with that? That makes sense." Scott thought aloud.

"Well...sort of." Christian continued, "Usually index fossils, ones that are usually found in a particular stratum, are used as the index or indicator." Christian paused to see if they were following him and then continued, "According to scientists, the problem is that sometimes index fossils are found in strata where they shouldn't be."

"Actually, the geologic column, where many of the index fossils are charted, were dated years before radiometric dating methods were invented," Scott defended.

"I agree," Christian nodded his head, popping a chip into his mouth. "But many scientists still hold to the original dates, even if they are not supported by the age-dating methods, which we know cannot be used for millions of years effectively. The Coelacanth fish is one of the best-known examples.

"Isn't that the fish that is alive, but they thought was extinct?" Anna asked.

"What!" Kayla exclaimed.

"Yes, she's right. The fossils of this fish are found only in rocks older than what evolutionists age-date as seventy million years. That is, if you assume the geologic time scale is real. But living Coelacanth fish have been found in the Indian Ocean!" Christian announced.

"No way!" Scott said, incredulously.

"What I like is that evolutionists call them 'living fossils' for lack of a better explanation," Anna added.

"How can it be a fossil and still be alive? I would think that meant it wasn't extinct in the first place." Kayla said.

"I agree, Kayla. So, what does that tell you about the validity of the age-dating methods?" Christian asked.

"Doesn't sound very scientific to me," Kayla said, gingerly eating her soup.

"Which do you like better archaeology or paleontology?" Scott asked, as he eyed the dessert menu.

"What's the difference? Ancient stuff is ancient stuff," Kayla queried.

"Actually the two are quite different, and I'm not sure which I like better at this point. Archaeology mainly deals with artifacts, and paleontology deals with all preserved life forms from bacteria to whales to dinosaurs," Christian said as he flipped through the book Anna had handed him. "Hey listen to this . . . here's a legend of a world-wide flood."

"Flood? As in Noah and the animals?" Kayla asked with one delicately-shaped eyebrow arched in disbelief. " You're kidding."

Anna's heart sank. She had heard this remark before. She knew an argument could quickly end their budding friendship and she sincerely hoped if there were differences they could be discussed rationally.

"Yes," Christian said his dark eyes flashing. "As in Noah and the flood beginning in Genesis chapter 6:9"

"You actually believe that story to be true?" Kayla asked, already bored with the conversation and wanting to return to shopping.

"We believe it's a historical account that it actually happened," Anna responded.

Kayla snapped to attention, " Not you, too!"

Scott, set down the dessert menu, with all thoughts of his stomach forgotten, "Kayla and I believe God created the world, but much of Genesis reflects an allegorical genre."

Christian responded not unkindly, "We believe it reflects facts, the way things really happened. If God didn't expect us to take the Bible literally, then why have a Bible at all?"

"And why would He make the first book of the Bible the one we wouldn't take literally?" Anna added.

"That doesn't make sense," Christian nodded. "Besides Genesis 11 is the account of Abraham, who is the beginning of the Davidic line and leads to the lineage of Christ. All Christians take that literally, and it's a major part of Genesis."

Kayla huffed, "Well, we do take some parts of it literally, just not the six days and 'poof' all was created part."

"Are you saying that you pick and choose what parts of the Bible you want to believe?" Anna questioned.

Not knowing how to answer the question, Scott said, "Whatever you believe is fine with me, but taking Genesis literally is not widely agreed upon, even among Christians. And not all Christians believe in a world-wide Flood, not to mention the scientific community, which holds to the view of a localized flood. In fact, the flooding reported in legends was very possibly resigned to a small geographic locality."

"That reminds me of a cartoon I saw. God promised Noah after the Flood that He would never send another flood to destroy the world. If he meant a localized flood, then He has lied, since we all know that there have been many localized floods around the world!" Christian paused, then continued, "For God to stand by His word, He had to mean a world-wide Flood."

"I see what you mean, but Scott should know what he is talking about. He has a master's degree in physics," Kayla offered.

"This has nothing to do with physics," Scott glared at his sister, uncomfortable with his credentials being mentioned. "I believe that God created the world, but not necessarily as stated in Genesis. He could have done it that way if He chose, but He could have done it through evolution too. All this can be proven through scientific means."

"Evolution or science for that matter doesn't have any definite proof." Anna flatly stated. "Both evolution and creation are belief systems. I mean no one was there at the time of creation, although Jesus refers to the book of Genesis several times in the New Testament. To believe God created the world is taken on faith. To believe that the universe was started by some other unknown mechanism takes faith."

Kayla huffed, "How did we get on this topic anyway? I don't want to talk about evolution, I'd rather be shopping."

"The topic came up because of this book." Christian held up the hardback book.

Scott asked, "How do you reconcile dinosaurs with the flood? Did they climb aboard the ark?" He didn't share his sister's indifference; he was very interested in the topic.

"The average size of a dinosaur was the same as a dog or a chicken. Many of the larger dinosaurs could have boarded as juveniles, when they were much smaller. What most people don't comprehend is the size of the ark. It was huge!" Christian said.

"Do you remember the dimensions?" Anna asked. "I know I've read about them, something about cubits, which I know means the length of a forearm."

"Hmm, that would mean about seventeen or eighteen inches," Scott surmised.

"Yes, that's right, around seventeen and a half inches. The ark was thought to be about 438 feet long, 73 feet wide, and 44 feet high. There would have been plenty of room for two of each kind. And we know there are plenty of variations within a species. Not every variation needed to be on board, just two of each kind."

"Great. Then when the ark landed, all the baby dinos walked out and lived happily ever after with man. How come we don't have dinosaur stories in our history?" Scott asked, still not convinced.

"That's a good question. While we don't have dinosaur stories or legends, we do have..." Christian began flipping through the book, "many legends of dragons."

"Dragons! You're not going to tell me that dragons were on the ark too?" Kayla asked with a giggle. Looking at Anna, then Christian and seeing their serious faces, she couldn't help herself, and she began laughing, "Now I've heard everything!"

Chapter 14
Modern Day Dragons!

"That's not what he means." Anna stuck up for Christian. "He means that throughout the ages, people have had dragon stories. These creatures could have been dinosaurs that existed at the time. The word 'dinosaur' wasn't coined until the 1800's."

"Well, you're right. There are dragon legends, but how does that fit in with dinosaurs?" Scott asked, really interested. "Hey, let's order dessert, this may take a while."

Grinning, Christian agreed, while the girls declined. "He thumbed through the book and said, "Here! It talks about dragon legends and the description seems to be more like dinosaurs than dragons.

"Here's a Sumerian story dating back to 3000 BC. It tells about a hero named Gilgamesh who fought a huge dragon and cut off his head. Here's another story set in England — the story of St. George who slew a dragon that lived in a cave."

The waitress brought two ice cream sundaes, setting them before the boys. After thanking her, they continued their conversation.

"Well, we've already established that there are dragon stories. We Asians are famous for them," Scott grinned.

"Great. Now we are talking about ancient Chinese legends as truth! This is too much," Kayla exclaimed. She took her spoon and helped herself to her brother's ice cream sundae. "Oooo, that hurts!" Kayla clapped a hand to her jaw. She cringed as the cool dessert caused her new filling to smart.

"That's what you get for stealing my dessert without asking," Scott teased. He good naturally grinned, "Want some more?"

Kayla ignored him. "Yes, there are many Chinese stories about dragons. In fact, we know many, but they're pagan legends. Dragon remains haven't been found, but dinosaur remains have," she insisted stubbornly.

"I should back up and explain what the name 'dinosaur' actually means. It came about in 1841 by Sir Richard Owen, a famous anatomist. It means 'fearfully-great lizard.' Over time it has been shortened, and many people think it means 'terrible-lizard.' After examining the remains of several dinosaurs, he coined the word. That doesn't mean he discovered the creature, only that he gave it a name. He couldn't explain the fossilized creatures and so the name he coined seemed to fit. Dinosaurs could have been called dragons in ancient times. Besides a dinosaur named the *Baryonyx* fits the description of a dragon. Its name means, *heavy claw*."

"But you were claiming the Bible as a reference," Scott said. "Where does it mention dinosaurs in the Bible?"

"It doesn't use the actual word, obviously. If it did, we wouldn't be having this conversation. What is mentioned, depending on your Biblical translation, is the word 'dragon,' which in Hebrew is *tannim*. This word appears at least twenty-one times. There are passages in the Bible about dragons that lived on the land and in the sea." Christian smiled as he ate another spoonful of his ice cream sundae. "Mmm tastes great."

"Christian, tell them about the references to *Leviathan*." Anna reminded him.

"In the book of Job, Chapter 41, it talks about a great animal, that lived in the sea. Its name was *Leviathan,* and it may have even breathed fire and smoke."

"I'm not a biology major," Scott said, "but technically the *Plesiosaur* or other sea creatures are not categorized under the dinosaur phylum."

"Yes, you're right. The *Plesiosaur,* while in the *class* of reptilia, the same class as the dinosaur, is in the *family* of Cryptocleididae. I was just indicating places in Scripture that mentioned creatures that could be similar to those found in the fossil record."

"If you look at the way dragons are mentioned in the Scriptures, it could only describe what we call dinosaurs today," Anna said.

"Like what?" Kayla asked, interested despite herself.

"Well, in Job, the Scripture talks about *behemoth*, which is described as having a tail like a cedar and bones like bars of iron, and chief, or impressive in the creative ways of God. This has been interpreted, erroneously by some Bible scholars as an animal like an elephant or hippopotamus."

"Those animals certainly don't have a tail like cedar trees," Kayla laughed.

"Exactly!" Anna said, proud of her new friend, "Can you think of an animal that does?"

"I think this is a loaded question," Kayla said, knowing she was being set up. "Don't tell me. A dinosaur, right?"

"It does sound more like the animal that was described in Job," Anna replied, "doesn't it?"

"Yes, it does," Kayla admitted. "I'm going to read that chapter again on my own."

"There really isn't much of a mystery when it comes to dinosaurs if you look at Scripture," Anna said. "We know they were created on the sixth day, along with other land animals and man. They were still able to get to places like China and England because the land mass was believed to be one."

Christian added, "Many dinosaurs died, due to the changes in their environment, after the Flood, unless you count those that may have been in the deepest jungles waiting to be found."

"You think dinosaurs still live?" Scott asked, intrigued by

the notion.

"Not in the sense of *T. rex* running around, but there have been reports of unusual sightings not that long ago," Christian responded.

"Let's talk about the Flood some more. You think forty days of rain caused the earth to change dramatically, but I find that hard to believe," Scott said. "Besides, in all my studies I've been immersed in evolutionary beliefs. Evolution is a given for any serious scientist."

"I've studied evolution too, but along with creationist beliefs. We can get into the specifics of the Flood another time. For now, keep in mind that it was a cataclysmic flood with the 'fountains of the deep' opening, probably volcanoes erupting, and much more. But I want to leave you with something to consider, before we bore Kayla to death," Christian said, smiling to soften his words.

Anna looked at Kayla and Scott, knowing what her brother was going to ask them to consider and trying to gauge their openness to hear his next words. She inwardly sighed, not knowing them well enough and, if looks were all she had to go on, neither looked outwardly receptive. She silently prayed that Christian's words would be seeds that fall on fertile soil.

"If we look at life with evolutionary eyes, in other words, the world began however it began, and okay," Christian held up his hand knowing what Scott would say, "even if you believe God began the world with evolution..." He waited to see Scott nod his head.

"Okay, even if God created the world with evolution, in the Scriptures God says, 'everything He created was good.' How could death, before there was sin in the world be good?" Christian waited, pausing for his words to sink in.

"I don't get it! What does death have to do with anything?" Kayla asked.

"Death, as in the result of sin from the story of Adam and Eve?" Scott asked, seeing where Christian was headed.

"Yes," Christian clarified for Kayla, "If what God created was good and there was no sin yet before the fall, when

Adam and Eve sinned, then it makes sense that there should not have been death until after sin. So, all animals and men lived together in harmony until there was sin."

"God did not intend for man to die. Death is a consequence of sin." Anna reiterated.

"So," Scott said, thinking out loud, "if you believe in evolution, you believe man evolved from animals. In essence you are saying there is death all along because things would have lived, and then died from natural selection and changes in structures as they evolved. Hmm. I've never thought of it that way."

"In Genesis 3:21 it states that the first death of an animal occurred when God shed the blood of an animal in the garden and clothed Adam and Eve. It is difficult for me to believe that blood was shed before sin," Christian said, then added, "After Jesus died for our sins and paid the price, in a complete and free submission to the will of His Father, he conquered death, and so opened up the possibility of salvation to all men. The obedience of Jesus transformed the curse of death into a blessing."

"I still don't see what this has to do with dinosaurs," Kayla said with a frown.

"Evolutionary belief is that dinosaurs lived millions of years before man. They lived and died before man was even around. There is no empirical proof. In other words proof that is verifiable or provable. But we do have the Scriptures and what they reveal through God's word."

No one said anything for several moments. Scott finally broke the silence as he beckoned to the nearby waitress, "Check, please."

112

Chapter 15
Birds of a Feather

"If you think I'm big, you should see God." The words were emblazoned under the picture of the dinosaur on Christian's long sleeved shirt. Anna and Christian eagerly set out for the dig early Thursday morning. This was why they had come in the first place, to photograph a *T. rex* dig in progress. What they weren't expecting when they arrived was the less than friendly reception awaiting them.

Christian set down their equipment, smiling over at Dr. Lane. "Good morning!"

Dr. Lane walked over, and read the words frowning. He returned the greeting with a sneer, "So, the little misinformed creationists have come to take pictures of our dinosaur." His sarcasm was not lost on the Murphys. It was a definite change over a few days ago when Dr. Lane had courteously showed them around the site.

Deciding not to answer, Anna busied herself with arranging her photography equipment. After the discussion with Kayla and Scott, she felt drained. Defending her beliefs was something she took seriously, yet wanting to maintain their friendship was also important to her. While they had parted on friendly terms, things were a bit strained as each considered what had been discussed.

Anna carefully attached the 100 mm macro lens she would use for her first close up shots. Christian, on the other hand, had been inspired by the talk that they had with the Song Les. He loved discussing creationist beliefs and readily rose to the challenge.

"Why do you think we are misinformed, sir?" Christian politely inquired, knowing it was better to be courteous in any discussion rather than confrontational. He did wonder if perhaps he had pushed it a bit by wearing the shirt.

"You have been home-educated and sheltered. There is a big world out there with more scientific information than you can imagine. I am sure that you haven't been exposed to most of it," Dr. Lane stated, taking off his glasses and cleaning them before replacing them.

"We have been immersed in science even before we could read. Our father has a degree in biology and a doctorate in archaeology," Anna interjected, wanting Dr. Lane to know that he was not the only one who held a doctorate in ancient studies.

"Yes, I am well aware of Dr. Murphy's contributions to the field until he went over to the dark side," Dr. Lane said.

"The dark side?" Christian asked with raised eyebrows. He knew, however, that Dr. Lane was referring to creation science as an evil, which would have been laughable in any other circumstance.

"Yes. When your father earned his doctorate, he wrote papers with the acknowledgement that there were many unknown factors in evolution."

"I can't believe my father believed in evolution," Anna stated, her photography equipment forgotten as she gaped open-mouthed in dismay. From her earliest years she could remember being taught that the Bible contained the written, inerrant word of God, and that the Genesis account was to be taken literally.

"I didn't say he wrote on evolution in the sense that he understood its mechanism," Dr. Lane said in a huff, "he wrote a paper stating that there were many aspects of evolution that were undiscovered *as yet*." He emphasized the last two words.

"In other words, evolution cannot be proven through the scientific method," Christian clarified flatly. "Anna, Dad got his degree years ago, most of the creation foundations and organizations we now take for granted, like the Institute for Creation Research and Answers in Genesis, were not in place at that time. Dad's degree was from a state university and while he believed the creation account, he had to choose his words wisely when writing his doctorate dissertation."

"We are not here to discuss your father's credentials," Dr. Lane dismissed, "only his apparent lack of teaching you both sides of the coin. You know there is a very tiny segment of the world that puts any stock in your creationist belief."

"I'd like to see your statistics," Christian sighed, pulling off his baseball cap and repositioning it. "Simply saying that only a small segment of the population believes in creation and using that as the sole basis of your argument, doesn't convince me that I should change my beliefs."

"Yeah!" Anna agreed enthusiastically. "Besides, Dr. Lane, we have studied about evolution, and we find it more about a belief system than scientific fact."

Dr. Lane chuckled. "And the same could be said about creation. It is after all, based on *your* belief system." He was enjoying this exchange more than he cared to admit. His purpose as a professor had been to educate young people and, as with these two, he often found preconceived notions and religious beliefs a hindrance that needed retooling.

"Well, let's begin our discussion with the geologic column. It shows the vertical order of geologic time zones laid down over millions of years. Are you familiar with this scientifically recorded layering of strata where fossilized remains are found all over the world?" Dr. Lane peered at them as he pulled up a folding chair, making himself comfortable and signaling for the two to take seats nearby.

Anna inwardly groaned. She brought her backpack with her as she sat down on a boulder. *I wanted to take pictures of Pete's dragon, not get into an evolution vs. creation science debate,* Anna thought. She could at least ready her equipment as she listened. She could see the enthusiasm in Christian's face as he quickly followed suit and took a seat.

Not waiting for an answer Dr. Lane continued, "Well, the geologic column shows an excellent example of the stages of evolutionary life over millions of years. I can't imagine any clearer example. You see, the geologic column contains twelve major systems, each comprised and identified by the different kinds and numbers of fossils."

"Yes, I am well aware of the textbook version of the geologic column," Christian asserted, "yet there is much disagreement as to whether the geologic column can actually be found in its entirety other than in a textbook."

"Of course the column can be found in, well, in many places in the world. It's been documented," Dr. Lane blustered. Yet he was not forthcoming with the names of these places.

"I do know that many geologic sites around the world, such as Grand Canyon, show layers of the geologic column to be missing," Christian further stressed, "How can millions of years be missing?"

"Yes, well, that can happen. The Grand Canyon appears to be an unexplained mystery. I am sure we will find a reason for it in the future," Dr. Lane said dismissively. Apparently missing layers were not a problem to his evolutionary doctrine. "In the geologic column, the fossils show the process of evolution from its simple beginnings to its more complex forms. This can be seen by anyone with half a brain." Dr. Lane waved his hand pointing toward Luke as an example. Luke was busy hammering a stubborn slab of sedimentary rock, trying to break it apart. He could not hear all of their discussion, but he had a good idea of what was being said.

"If there was a gradual evolution from simple invertebrates to complex organisms, shouldn't we find transitional fossils?" Anna asked quietly. She already knew the answer. She

116

and her brother had been involved in a Peace River dig where a transition from ape to man had supposedly been found.

"Ah, the *coup de grâce* the creationists always use... where are the transitional fossils? Well, my young friends, many transitions exist, and there is much evidence of this today. Do you actually think dinosaurs are extinct? Think again! Dinosaurs have evolved into birds."

Anna ignored the ridiculous comment while Christian laughed. "Are you talking about transitions from simple to complex being found in the geologic column? You yourself said it was a prime example of evolution taking place. If this is true, where are the undisputable facts?"

Anna admired the way her brother had brought the discussion back to her original question. "Yes, where are the fossilized remains of transitions found?"

"Well, of course it is well known that *Archaeopteryx* is a transition from reptile to bird," Dr. Lane looked smug. He was not ready for Christian's response.

"Dr. Lane, the creature you mentioned is an ancient bird not a reptile," Christian responded.

"It is well documented that the *Archaeopteryx* has features similar to both reptiles and birds, which makes it an evolutionary link between the two creatures," Dr. Lane replied. "Doesn't that make sense to you?"

"From what I have read, the *Archaeopteryx* was found in the same strata as regular birds. Therefore it could not have been a transitional form that evolved into a bird. *Archaeopteryx* is just a special kind of bird that no longer exists. That's what makes sense to me," Christian countered.

"Dr. Lane do you really believe that *Archaeopteryx* evolved into a *T. rex*? Anna asked.

"Yes, I do." Dr. Lane responded. "I guess it all depends on how you look at it and obviously you are seeing it differently than I am." Dr. Lane looked annoyed. "Nevertheless, people incorrectly assume that dinosaurs are extinct, when in fact more than 8,000 living species of dinosaurs exist."

"How can that be?" Anna asked.

"Birds are the direct descendants of meat-eating dinosaurs, and under modern biological classifications they are considered to be a subset of the Dinosauria. The earliest fossil bird, *Archaeopteryx*, which came from the late Jurassic rocks in Germany. It looks like a small, meat-eating dinosaur, and would never have been identified as a bird if its feathers had not been preserved."

"Not all biologists agree with the dinosaur-to-bird link." Christian refused to be persuaded. "In fact the minority, not the majority, of biologists would agree with you."

"That's not correct, but as you said so eloquently earlier, numbers, are not going to convince me."

Anna inwardly groaned. Apparently Christian's words had been taken to heart and then used against them. "Let me see if I understand what you are trying to tell us, Dr. Lane," Anna said, "You believe that it took millions of years for dinosaurs to turn into birds and in the meantime this *Archaeopteryx* evolved into a half-bird half-dinosaur creature."

"Yes," Dr. Lane smiled, he was pleased, for he thought that he had finally made some headway.

"You also believe that this half-bird half-dinosaur became a bird millions of years later."Anna watched as he nodded his assent. "Well, if that is true, how could a half-bird half-dinosaur coexist with other birds?"

"Well, one theory is that they are from a different species of dinosaurs. Some were as small as chickens, that gradually evolved over millions of years and transitioned into birds," Dr. Lane said.

"Two different evolutionary family trees leading to the same type of animal form doesn't make sense to me," Anna replied.

"I agree with Anna," Christian said. "The anatomical structures between reptiles and birds are too different. Just look at the structure of a bird, especially its lungs, air sacs and hollow bones and the way it was built for flight. It couldn't possibly happen."

"Yes, but with millions of years of time, the evolutionary process caused the changes," Dr. Lane continued his mantra.

"Dr. Lane, I'm afraid we must agree to disagree," Anna

interrupted. May I please take some photos now?"

"By all means," Dr. Lane acquiesced rising from his chair and leading the way, "Follow me. But I must warn you, your attitude needs changing!"

Chapter 16
Simple or Complex?

"Let's take a closer look at Pete's dinosaur shall we?" Dr. Lane was firmly in control.

"Do you think I can begin photographing?" Anna asked.

"Go right ahead." Dr. Lane began walking closer to the fossilized bones of the gigantic dinosaur.

The Murphys were awestricken as they gazed at the outline of the bones that were carefully being freed from their rocky enclosure.

Dr. Lane gestured to where the workers were careful to chisel and chip the area around the bones, brushing away residue as they worked. Pete was enormous.

"What can you tell us about Pete's dragon?" Anna asked, snapping her camera as she spoke.

"Don't you mean dinosaur?" Dr. Lane frowned, the pun not lost on him.

"Sorry." Anna turned her head, hiding her smile.

"As I told you several days ago, we think it is over forty-five feet long, the longest found to date. We believe it will stand over twenty-five feet tall and will weigh about eight tons. The skull is five and a half feet in length."

"Doesn't *Tyrannosaurus rex* mean 'tyrant lizard king'?" asked Christian.

"Yes, it was named because of its fearsome teeth, which made it a ferocious meat-eater." Dr. Lane adjusted the wide-brimmed hat as he tilted his head back for a better view.

"Don't you think it's possible that its teeth were designed for eating special types of foods such as melons, coconuts, and other large seed pods?" Christian asked.

"I guess it could possibly eat those things along with meat. Why do you ask?" Dr. Lane asked with a puzzled expression.

"Because, according to our beliefs that is before the fall, we believe that it wouldn't have killed its prey to eat," Anna piped up.

"Let's not even go there," Dr. Lane fumed. "I've never seen teeth like a *Tyrannosaurus rex's* used in a herbivore. Have you?"

"There are animals such as the giant panda, gorillas, and fruit-eating bats with sharp teeth," Christian responded evenly.

Dr. Lane ignored his response. "As I was saying, other characteristics of this great animal are its short neck made of very thick vertebrae upon which large powerful muscles would have been needed to support its huge head."

"It is amazing," Anna agreed, taking a photograph of one of the staff brushing off the bones and another applying a thick layer of a type of gum sealant prior to the plaster coating.

"One puzzle remains in the size of its forearms, which seem small and useless since the *T. rex* can't reach the ground or its mouth with them," Dr. Lane said.

"You know, in some ways the *T. rex* reminds me of a kangaroo. Even though the kangaroo can reach its mouth with its hands, it has a similar shape," Anna said.

"And Kangaroos are herbivores. Many of the animals are similar because they have the same Creator," Christian responded to his sister's comment.

"Well, the kangaroo is warm-blooded and did not evolve from the dinosaur. There is controversy over whether dinosaurs are warm- or cold-blooded, although they are classified with cold-blooded Reptilia," Anna agreed.

The Murphys were sure that the arms had a purpose. They each knew that God must have created the *Tyrannosaurus rex* with the perfect size required to meet all its needs. Yet, neither made the comment not wanting to further antagonize Dr. Lane.

Dr. Lane further revealed, "As you can see, we haven't excavated most of the lower limbs as yet, but we are almost certain it is articulated."

"What do you plan to do with this fossil once it is completely excavated?" Anna asked.

"We hope to display it at the Natural History Museum in the university here," Dr. Lane proudly answered.

"I would like to talk more about the fossil record and when the dinosaurs appeared, but we'll leave the discussion for another time." Dr. Lane dismissed them walking away. "Go ahead, and finish up your pictures. If you would like, Christian, you can help your sister set up, then come find me and I'll give you work to do on the dig."

"That would be great sir, thank you." Christian beamed, glad to eventually have the chance to help.

Anna was equally thrilled to finally photograph Pete's dragon uninterrupted.

"This was a massive, awesome creature, even if it is encased in rock. Our God who created this creature is awe-inspiring," she commented privately to Christian.

"I agree," Christian said, as impressed as Anna by the sheer size of the bones. After setting up the tripod for Anna, Christian went to help Dr. Lane.

Dr. Lane gave Christian a chisel and pointed to a section of bone, "You can begin work there, let's see if you are as adept with tools."

Soon it was obvious that Dr. Lane was using the strategy of divide and conquer. Dr. Lane first walked over to where Anna was working, "It won't make you nervous if I watch? Will it?"

He asked more as a statement than a question.

"No, not at all," Anna said, as she steadily worked.

"You know," Dr. Lane said, "it is very obvious that time does cause change."

"Dr. Lane, I disagree. Time alone cannot cause change in structures *especially* since both are found as fossils and both are equally complex. Earlier we were discussing birds. How is a bird more complex than a dinosaur? It seems they are both equally animals."

"Nevertheless, evolution exists. Things become more complex; it is a fact," After watching Anna for a few minutes Dr. Lane left.

Anna grinned. Photography was almost as tedious as paleontology fieldwork and not too much fun to watch.

Dr. Lane walked over to Christian.

"You know, Christian time does cause change," Dr. Lane stated.

"Then how can you reconcile the Second Law of Thermodynamics?" Christian asked, as he carefully chiseled around the right side of the skull.

"What is there to reconcile? This law states that energy evens out all over the universe. So what?" Dr. Lane frowned.

"Well, do you agree that energy always moves toward a disorganized state?" Christian asked.

"Yes, the process is called entropy." Dr. Lane patiently lectured, "Heat, by itself, always flows from high to low temperature and spreads out evenly in all directions."

"So, hot things cool down, and cold things warm up, metal rusts, and things decay. Complex things become simple," Christian stated.

Dr. Lane laughed. "So," he chuckled, "that's where you are going with this."

"Yes," said Christian. "Evolution states that frogs become princes, which violates that law because things get disorganized not complex."

"You are something else," Dr. Lane shook his head. "You can't apply that law to evolution."

"Why not?" Christian asked puzzled.

"Well, because we know things become more complex over millions of years."

Christian, seeing that they were getting nowhere, launched into another question before Dr. Lane could speak. "How do you think the *Tyrannosaurus rex* ended up here?"

"That's an excellent question, Christian, but first a bit of history. Dinosaurs are usually found in only three systems, which are categorized within the Mesozoic Period. The three systems are, the Triassic, Jurassic, and Cretaceous. We believe this *Tyrannosaur*, Pete, lived 65-million years ago."

Anna walked over with her camera wanting to take a shot of Christian, "How have you age-dated the fossil?" Anna asked.

"We found a tuatara, an index fossil," Dr. Lane said. "As we already discussed an index fossil is usually found in the same layer at various geographic locations. Finding an index fossil allows us to figure out the age of a fossil. The tuatara became extinct during the Cretaceous Period."

"But, what if an index fossil is found in a layer where it isn't usually located? I have heard of this happening," Christian responded, while making a mental note to check into the tuatara that Dr. Lane had mentioned.

"Yes, well, it rarely happens. And, only in situations where the area was affected by a catastrophic event, that may have caused severe damage to the land, and thus jumbled the layers," Dr. Lane answered smoothly.

"A catastrophic event, such as a flood?" questioned Christian.

"Well... I guess that could be one possibility," Dr. Lane mumbled. "One reason we believe the bones are preserved is due to the likelihood of mineral-rich water over this area at one time. There are many springs in this region."

"Look! Christian shouted, as his chiseling revealed impressive teeth.

"My word, those are *T. rex* teeth! Hold it right there." Dr. Lane was excited in spite of himself. He immediately called for Luke, "I'm sorry Christian, but I'd like Luke to take over."

125

"No problem." Christian hid his disappointment at being prevented from continuing further. He walked to stand beside Anna.

Anna congratulated her brother, "Great find! Don't worry, I took some magnificent shots!"

"Thanks," her brother shrugged, "I better work on my research anyway, I'm unsure of the index fossil Dr. Lane mentioned earlier."

"Well, Christian, you better have an answer for him when he launches into his explanations of dinosaurs in the fossil record."

"Don't worry, Anna, I do. In every case, each basic type of dinosaur appears abruptly and without any in-between forms. For example, a gradual formation cannot be found for the spikes and plates in the Stegosaurus. So, I wonder what he will use to explain away the facts for this *T. rex*?" Christian asked, as he set up the tripod for his sister's use.

"I don't know, but I'm glad you know so much about the subject," Anna said. All she had to do was photograph the dinosaur and not defend its existence, which they both knew was thousands and not millions of years ago.

Chapter 17
A Long Way To Go

Anna stood and brushed off the knees of her jeans. She bent down and started unscrewing the camera from the tripod, knowing that she was finished for the day. In the past few hours, she had taken countless close-up pictures of the fossilized skull.

"I can't believe they've done this much in such a short time!" Anna commented.

Although the dig had been in process for less than six weeks, the bones were partly excavated, protruding from the rock face with some of the overburden chiseled away.

"Dr. Lane said they have been moving at an accelerated pace because of his specialized technique. Besides, from the little he has revealed, there appears to be big money backing this dig; both from the university and several private donors," Christian said.

"I wonder why? It's not like this is the first *T. rex* ever discovered." Removing the camera from the tripod, Anna placed it delicately inside one of the backpacks. Rummaging through the other pack, she extracted several heavily padded, black lens cases.

"What a day's work!" Christian said kneeling down beside Anna.

"This was great and so much fun. I hope Dad will be pleased with the pictures. I can't wait to see them developed!"

Christian nodded in agreement as he surveyed the site. Their only equipment besides the cameras, lens, and flash was a sturdy, black tripod that Christian had moved around several times for Anna. It was a letdown after Dr. Lane replaced him with Luke who was busy excavating the rest of the tooth. Christian thought it better to help Anna, rather than ask for another job. Setting up the tripod at varying heights and angles around the fossil allowed Anna to capture the dinosaur remains from different views.

Anna carefully placed all six rolls of exposed film into a waterproof clear bag.

Christian took off his baseball hat and wiped the sweat from his brow. Although the temperature was cool, the rigorous activity of moving supplies was keeping him warm. He had divided his time between helping Anna and watching the excavation.

Some of the fossils were so small that they were left in a block of rock to be separated in the lab. Others were being sprayed with resin, or painted with the PVA mixture which was similar to glue. Once the glue hardened it would protect the bone in transportation. The larger bone preparation was the most amazing to watch. Once a little more than half of the bone was freed from the rock, wet tissue paper was spread over the exposed surface to protect it. Then, strips of sackcloth were soaked in plaster and used to cover the surface in overlapping sections. When the plaster jacket hardened, the bone was carefully excavated and turned over. The same procedure was used on the other side.

While this was transpiring, Dr. Lane was carefully recording all these events and keeping an eye on the progress being made.

Anna had used an organizational technique for photographing these events that her father had taught her. The technique used was a planned approach for photographing a large still life. Dr. Murphy had used it successfully to alleviate the photographer's tendency to be overwhelmed with a whole scene and missing key points when randomly clicking away.

"Dad's technique is tedious, but I think I shot every inch of that exposed fossil!" Anna exclaimed.

Christian stopped working to lean against a rock. "Don't you ever get tired of taking a bunch of pictures?"

Anna smiled, "No, I did a lot of close-up and detailed work. The next time I come I'll get a broader view and then steadily work my way out." Anna swept her bangs off her forehead; she was tired, but elated by the day's work. The weather had been perfect, cool yet clear.

Christian and Anna worked silently side by side to pack the rest of the photography equipment into their padded backpacks.

Anna sat down to take a short break. She could finally take time to appreciate her surroundings. She sat down and looked around. The ledge, on which she sat, was east of the Continental Divide. It protruded from the mountain and dropped a little less than half-way down Diamond Peak. Lodgepole pines dominated the lower levels, higher up, in the subalpine ecosystem, the dominant trees were Douglas fir and Englemann spruce. The mountains were bathed in yellows, oranges, and reds by the setting sun.

"Wow! I can't believe how late it is," she exclaimed with surprise in her voice.

"You were pretty focused. Hey! No pun intended," Christian said, laughing at his own joke.

"Yeah, I guess I was. I can't believe most of the team left without us."

Now that the sun had begun to set behind the western mountains, the view of the sky was spectacular. Anna and Christian were used to the sunsets in Florida, but this surpassed that beauty. They hurried to finish their packing in the remaining light before the temperatures plummeted into the teens. Anna fastened her blue-gray jacket around her shoulders more securely to fight against the cooling temperatures.

"Let's go," Christian said as he lifted one of the loaded green backpacks onto his shoulders.

Christian left Anna with the rest of the gear and approached Dr. Lane.

The stocky man stood alone on the other side of the excavation site. Here, away from the roped-off area, stood a nylon tent and a small folding table. Beyond that, Dr. Lane leaned against a large bolder, deep in thought. He wasn't wearing his ever-present safari hat; this made his balding head all the more noticeable. He was holding and slowly speaking into a micro-cassette recorder. He seemed to be reading from some notes scribbled on a piece of paper, in front of him, anchored by a baseball sized rock.

Christian, slowed to a stop a short distance away. Christian's Uncle Mike, an archaeologist, once told him when he was too busy to keep a journal, he would document the day's events into a tape recorder. Christian assumed that Dr. Lane was doing the same.

The tall teen adjusted his Florida Marlin's baseball hat as he patiently waited for Dr. Lane to finish. Finally the cassette player was switched off, and Christian jumped at the opportunity to speak.

"Hi, Dr. Lane, sorry for interrupting. I just wanted to let you know that Anna and I are finished for today. Luke said to let you know we are heading up to camp. Remember? We are spending the night.

Dr. Lane didn't bother to look up; with annoyed impatience he nodded his head but didn't immediately make a reply. Making a few more notes on his paper, he finally waved Christian away. "Fine, fine. I don't care."

"Okay, good-night, sir," Christian said. He turned away without another word and stiffly walked back to where Anna was waiting.

"That man is not very pleasant," Christian said.

Anna nodded in agreement. Dr. Lane had been less than cordial to her as well, particularly after their earlier discussion about evolution, but she refrained from commenting.

130

"Hi guys! All finished?" Luke called as he approached the teens. He wore a wide, good-natured grin on his face, a nice change from Dr. Lane. "How'd the photographing go?"

Anna greeted Luke with a smile of her own. "It went great!" She chanced a quick glance at Christian. Her brother stuffed his hands in his pockets but didn't make a negative reply.

Anna went on, "The workers, for the most part, were friendly enough. I got some great pictures — exactly what I needed."

Christian grinned at his sister's enthusiasm and tried to change his attitude after his encounter with Dr. Lane. "This is an awesome paleontological discovery."

Anna, Luke, and Christian talked for a while longer.

"Well, I guess we'd better get going. Are we climbing or walking?" Christian teased his sister.

"What do you want to do?" Anna asked.

He stared at her with a shocked look. Anna couldn't help but smile. "Okay, that was a dumb question; of course you want to climb. That sounds good to me too."

They had taken the path the other day when the leg bone had broken. The trip had taken more than forty minutes to walk in the rain.

Anna and Christian shouldered their backpacks and made their way over to the ropes where they would begin their ascent.

Luke gathered some tools and papers. "I'll be ready in just a minute." Motioning back at Troy he continued. "I gave up staying as late as Troy, long ago. He's a rare breed, I've never known a man to work such long hours. I'm usually one of the last to go at the end of the day. But I always," he emphasized, "leave *before* Troy. My wife thinks I get home late enough." Luke smiled as his thoughts turned toward his family at home.

They talked while Luke carefully put his papers, drawings, and supplies into a mesh bag. After making sure the bag was secure, he slung the braided strap over his shoulder.

Luke removed a two-way radio clipped to his belt and radioed that they would soon be starting to climb. A static filled reply immediately followed.

A few minutes later, the orange-colored rope appeared. As Anna and Christian watched quietly, Dr. Lane came up from behind. Taking off his glasses he began to polish them as he said, "You know the technology used on this site is quite advanced."

Anna and Christian turned at the first sound of his voice, trying to hide their surprise, which was easy in the dimness of the diminishing light.

I wonder why he is being nice again? Anna thought.

Dr. Lane pointed up at the rope as it steadily moved. "Take this pulley system for example . . ." he went on to explain. Dr. Lane continued without noticing Christian and Anna's exchange of raised eyebrows. "The system can be set to simply help you climb, and it's a lot safer than climbing without a safety line," he motioned to several pieces of equipment lying on the ground. "As you ascend, the rope is rolled away with the help of a generator, making it virtually impossible for you to fall." He didn't give the Murphys a chance to ask why. "The reason for this is because no slack is left in the rope. If you happen to slip, the rope will hold you in the same place until you can find your footing."

How can someone be barely civil one minute and then decide to nicely explain a pulley system the next? Christian thought with confusion. *Dr. Lane just doesn't seem to make sense.* Christian shook his head, trying to clear his thoughts, as he, Luke, and Anna began to strap on the harnesses.

Christian, in a dark-blue harness and red helmet, waited for the okay to start the 200-foot climb to the top. Rappelling down the drop-off had been an adventure, yet he had also enjoyed ascending and knew he would enjoy this as well.

Anna looked up at the sharp incline of the mountain face, uncertainty etched across her own face; 200-feet was a long way up. A screech owl could be heard as it circled somewhere high above her. The sound of the eerie cry added to her feelings of apprehension. *I wish we didn't have to climb up in the dark,* Anna thought with dismay. *Lord, please help me.* She prayed, as she tightened her harness.

Suddenly a large, strategically placed, florescent floodlight pierced the darkness making the mountain and excavation site seem almost as light as day.

The gas-powered generator could faintly be heard as it rumbled. Christian was ready and would be the first in the group to ascend, which he didn't mind. He nimbly started up the sharp incline, but he was careful to take his time. He made it a point to carefully check each and every foot and handhold before placing his full weight on it. In less than ten minutes, Christian was one hundred feet up. Anna and Luke stood watching below as he steadily climbed.

Dr. Lane left them, mumbling something about having to go back to finish work. Anna and Luke, their heads tipped back, continued to watch Christian.

Christian stopped 130-feet up to rest and find another foothold. He was standing on a rock ledge that was a mere foot wide and protruded out about the same length. Catching his breath, for a moment Christian scanned the area and quickly found a route to the left where he could continue on.

The jagged edges of the rock face made the climb much easier than a smooth face would have, and it didn't take Christian long to be high overhead. Anna silently marveled at the unique mountain that looked as if thousands of ready-made hand and footholds had been purposely set in place. Perhaps they had. *Thank you Jesus that you know our needs even before we ask.*

Christian had a mere thirty-five feet to go before he reached the top. He dug his fingers into a crevice in an attempt to pull up. He used his left foot as a leverage to hoist his body onward. *I'm almost there,* Christian thought. In the middle of pulling up, he suddenly felt the rope go slack. Without the support of the rope to secure him, he immediately tried to steady himself. The muscular boy snatched at the closest thing he could. He clung to a protruding rock near his head. Christian immediately realized that he was clutching the rock in vain. The rock came loose. At the same time he lost his footing. Christian helplessly slipped downward!

Chapter 18
Safe?

Anna had heard a sound behind and had taken her eyes off Christian. Hearing Christian shout, she snapped her attention back and gasped. Clapping a hand to her mouth, she stood rooted to the spot in terror as she watched her brother slide down the rocky incline. The safety line, attached to the back of his harness, was useless as the severed end dropped down on top of him. He slipped down the face of the mountain, groping helplessly for a safe handhold, but now he found only loose rocks.

Anna finally found her voice. "What happened! Can't we do something to help him?" She pleaded to Luke.

Christian valiantly fought to slow his slide. If he fell backwards, the only thing that would stop his fall was the ledge far below. He frantically grasped at a rock, trying to slow down. He spotted a little outcropping no bigger then one and a half feet wide about ten feet below. It was his best hope for survival.

Luke yelled into the two-way radio, "The safety line is useless. Can't you lower another rope?"

A crackled reply was heard, then silence. Anna took her eyes off Christian, looking into the worried face of Luke.

"What did he say?" she asked, hopes rising.

"Simon said he's lowering another rope, but it takes time!" Luke fumed.

"Troy! Get over here!" Luke yelled.

Dr. Lane was surprised at the uncharacteristic tone and snapped, "What's your problem?" He stopped in dismay as he watched Christian slide downward.

Oof! Christian fell upon a small ledge full of loose rocks and dirt. Still traveling fast his shoes hit the ledge and slid right off. He made a frantic grab for the ledge before he broke completely free, feeling himself slipping.

His body swaying, Christian held onto the small protrusion by his fingertips. He knew he wouldn't be able to hold on much longer. His arms already ached from abrasions he suffered on the way down.

He cried out to the Lord and surrendered his life to Him. Then, his fingertips gave way. Anna looked on in shock from 125 feet below. She couldn't watch her brother fall to his death! Anna covered her eyes, shoulders shaking. She silently screamed heavenward for mercy. Just then, Luke let out a whoop; Christian had slid down about twenty-five feet more when his bleeding fingers caught onto another, larger ledge.

Christian heaved in a lung full of air as he hung onto the two-foot ledge. Below him was a hundred feet of empty space. If he fell now, it would be all over. He would land right at the feet of Anna and Luke.

"Oh, Christian!" Anna was near tears. "Can't we climb up to get him?"

Dr. Lane looked at Luke with utter disgust. "This is all your fault! You should have climbed up first!"

"I don't see how that would have helped. The safety line broke loose," Luke looked puzzled. He turned his gaze to Anna, but could think of nothing to do that would be quick enough to save the young man's life. He wordlessly placed a hand on Anna's shoulder. He could offer her only comfort and prayer. He squeezed

Anna's shoulder gently and said, "Keep on praying."

Anna had not stopped praying since the first moment she had seen Christian slip; but, she bowed her head again as Luke lifted the situation up to Jesus.

Christian hung there in the same spot for the next several minutes. To those watching, the minutes seemed to pass like hours. Christian tried to catch his breath and come up with a plan. His eyes frantically roamed the face of the mountain, trying unsuccessfully to find an easy way to pull himself up onto the rock outcropping from which he hung.

"What's he doing?" Dr. Lane huffed.

Luke wheeled around to face him. "Trying to save his life."

Helplessly Anna asked, "How could the rope break? Why can't someone do something?" She pointed up to the form of Christian as he hung onto the ledge above. The florescent lights made his motionless body look pale and lifeless.

"Christian! You can do it!" Anna yelled encouragement.

"They're trying to lower another rope," Luke yelled, "hold on!"

Christian heard shouts, but was unaware of what was going on below. He inhaled with deep, slow breaths. He had only one solution. He gradually started to swing his lower body from side to side, knowing that he only had one chance to do this correctly.

"What's he doing?" Dr. Lane grumbled.

No one answered the question. They watched in suspense.

Christian waited until he had enough momentum before he finally swung his right leg up onto the ledge. The heel of his hiking boot caught onto the ledge and stayed. With a grunt of exertion he pulled himself up with all of his might. His muscles strained as he heaved himself, backpack, and all, up onto the ledge.

"Make the call!" Luke shoved the two-way radio into Troy's hand. "You're the boss—order them to hurry!"

Dr. Lane placed the two-way radio close to his month, he shouted. "Get that rope down here now!" he ordered.

On his knees, Christian slowly dragged himself to a

standing position, pressing himself against the rock face for stability. Praise God, he was safe for the moment and could catch his breath.

Anna smiled and wanted to shout with relief. *God is in control. He is our refuge and strength, a very present help in trouble.* Then her nagging thoughts broke into her happiness. *Would he make it all the way to the top without a safety rope to help?* Anna wanted to yell in frustration, but stubbornly refused to give in to the helpless temptation.

"There's no way he can make it without a rope!" Dr. Lane said bluntly. He shook his head in denial. "Especially in the dark."

The temperatures had plummeted with the sunset, and now the winds had picked up. It would be difficult for Christian to find his way, even with floodlights. The shadow would play tricks on his eyes.

Christian needed a plan. Somehow he knew he would get no assistance. Survival was in God's hands now. *Help me do it Lord! I know you are able to do far more abundantly than all we ask or think.* He prayed. He momentarily thought about leaving his expensive backpack, but decided against it. He inwardly promised that he would make it backpack and all.

It's a walk in the park, just a mere hundred feet, or so and I'll be at the top. Just don't look down. I can do all things in Christ who strengthens me. Christian quoted Scripture to give him strength and kept his mind on the present, concentrating on putting one hand and one foot in front of the other. He wouldn't let himself think about how badly his fingers were burning or let himself wonder why the rope broke in the first place. Christian started to ascend slowly, only twice as carefully as before, for now he had no safety line.

Anna was tired of helplessly waiting and pacing around. Nor did she want to make her own risky climb in the semi-darkness. There was, another way to the top. The dirt trail! This weaving, snake-like path sharply headed uphill all the way to the top. Anna wanted to be at the campsite for when, not if, Christian made it.

"I'm taking the trail," Anna announced, surprising the two

men.

Luke took his eyes off Christian and nodded approval. "I'm going too!" he agreed.

Dr. Lane looked from Anna and Luke to Christian's back. "I'll stay here."

Anna scrounged for her flashlight and she and Luke headed toward the trail. Finally, the long-awaited sound of the generator could be heard as it was switched on to full power.

Christian made a thirty-five foot gain by the time he heard the generator roar to life. *Maybe they're going to finally lower a rope!* Christian thought with relief. Meanwhile he scanned the rocks as he picked his way, pulling with all his might one second, and then desperately looking for a foothold the next. He used all his resources to keep climbing.

Only seconds after they first heard the generator a looped rescue knot seemed to drop out of the sky. A yell of excitement from Dr. Lane stopped Anna and Luke. They began to turn back to the ledge but stopped when they heard Dr. Lane shouting. Anna turned watching the swiftly descending rope. Her rising hopes were quickly dashed, as in disbelief she saw the rope miss Christian by more than fifty feet to the right. Anna couldn't stand to watch him struggling. She wordlessly followed Luke on the trail, keeping her flashlight trained on the ground. His long powerful strides were hard to keep up with as she trotted along. The bright flashlight barely cut through the darkness that surrounded them.

Meanwhile, Dr. Lane yelled into the two-way radio, tapping his foot in irritation. "Move the rope to the left!"

Several minutes later the rope had slowly, started shifting toward Christian. It was now only about fifteen feet out of reach.

Time seemed to crawl by while Dr. Lane yelled orders into the two-way radio. Anna and Luke made their way along the twisted trail, as Christian climbed up, vainly trying to reach the rope.

I'm almost there! The exhausted boy thought with relief. Christian, once again was only thirty-five feet from reaching the top.

With their adrenaline pumping, Luke and Anna silently hiked the trail in less than half the usual time. When they arrived at the top, Anna was devastated to find that Christian was still struggling to ascend. They immediately ran to the edge, which was crowded with other staff members. Anna, following Luke's lead, dropped to her stomach and scooted out. From this angle, the floodlights below shed an eerie glow. All they could make out was Christian's dark silhouette and the neon-colored rope.

Luke jumped up wanting to help Simon with the rope. Anna, however, stayed where she was. *Come on, Christian,* Anna thought with desperation, *you can do it! Lord, please help him.*

Twenty-five feet from the top Christian became stranded. There was nowhere left to climb, that he could see. The wall above him appeared to be sheer flat granite. His eyes darted to the right, hoping and praying that the rope would be close enough to grab. It wasn't. A volley of small stones tumbled down toward Dr. Lane. He avoided them with some difficulty, but was not hurt.

Christian, valiantly tried to find new footholds for his feet. The rope was almost close enough for him to reach.

Anna held her breath, not wanting to watch, and yet unable to turn away. She continued to cry out to the Lord.

Christian's fingers could not quite reach the rope. He could no longer hang on. Losing his grip, he tried one last desperate attempt. Christian flung himself toward the rope, extending his right arm as far as it would go. *A leap of faith,* he whispered to himself. *God help me!*

Chapter 19
Startling Information

Gravity worked against him and pulled downward. At that moment, his hand came into contact with . . . the stony wall, and a handhold! He immediately grabbed onto it as his fall was halted. He hung there, once again on the side of the mountain. Pain shot through his shoulder, but he was grateful to be alive. His feet searched and found another footrest.

The sheer will for survival had driven Christian forward. Grasping tightly with his other hand he held on for dear life. He didn't look for the rope again. He continued to search, finding hand and foot holds as he slowly, but steadily, made the climb to the top.

"You're doing it Christian, keep going!" Anna yelled down. She turned and jumped to her feet. Anna ran to stand beside Luke. The group of onlookers watched incredulously as Christian seemed to scale the remaining summit almost effortlessly as if a Divine hand were leading him. A few minutes later, everyone cheered when Christian reached safety. Anna ran tearfully and embraced her brother.

Christian grinned at the jubilant group around him. He felt exhausted and exhilarated, as he awkwardly patted his sister on the back. "One big step for man, but one small miracle for God!"

*   *   *   *   *   *   *   *   *

Christian fell into his sleeping bag that night exhausted from his ordeal. When he woke the next morning every muscle, even some he didn't know he had, ached. He rolled over and snuggled into his sleeping bag. He thanked God for saving his life. He could hear the sounds of the camp coming alive as the others were readying for the days work. He savored the smell of brewing coffee and bacon frying.

"Wake up, sleeping ugly," Anna teased. She was standing wide-awake in front of his tent, her normal cheerful self.

Christian opened one eye to glimpse her dressed in jeans and a bright blue ski sweater.

"Go away, I'm dying," Christian moaned.

Anna laughed, "So sorry to hear that. Guess I'll have to eat all the bacon."

"Did you say bacon?" Christian raised his head a fraction of an inch to stare at his sister, and then laid back down groaning again.

Anna closed the flap, walked to where the breakfast was and offered to help. She knew it would be several minutes before Christian would be joining her. While she had bandaged and treated Christian's superficial wounds late yesterday, she, too, thanked God for the gift of life. Anna was relieved that yesterday's incident had ended happily.

Still Anna was concerned about finding the cause of the severed rope. The town authorities had been notified along with the Park rangers since there was suspicion that the rope had been purposefully cut. Although there was no definite proof, they were reasonably certain that the person who cut the rope and the

142

environmentalist were one and the same: a certain Lawrence Edelman. The same telltale calling card had been left, a poisonous yellow buttercup.

Christian walked stiffly into camp, and breakfast began with a lively discussion about who cut the rope. Then the conversation drifted to dinosaurs, particularly the cause of the extinction of dinosaurs. Two of the five-man team working on Pete all were students, or graduates, of the paleontology program at nearby university. They drove up early each morning, except for Rick and Luke who lived nearby, Dr. Lane, who stayed in the trailer, and Simon who camped on occasion.

"I still believe in the gradual extinction theory," Rick Lane huffed.

"There is no way that theory holds up any longer. I can't imagine anyone still believes dinosaurs died over a period of millions of years due to climate, sea-level variations, or volcanoes," Clark Wallace, a graduate, sipped his coffee. "We now know that there is exciting evidence substantiating past speculation on a catastrophe occurring because of an asteroid. The iridium level in craters is evidence."

"I agree; however, I lean toward a varied extinction theory, such as a cataclysmic event like an asteroid, along with geographic and climatically varying changes, over sixty-five million years ago," said Carlos Ramirez a second-year graduate student. "I don't think many scientists still hold to the single-event theory."

"We're talking about the great unsolved mystery," Clark stated. "Let's face it. We just don't know what caused the extinction of the creatures, or if they all died out at the same time, on all continents. The K/T boundary marks the extinction, but it's clearly not of all species."

"The K/T boundary?" Anna questioned. Anna smiled at Christian who had taken a seat next to her on the picnic bench, with a plate full of bacon and eggs. He looked tired, but that didn't seem to have any effect on his appetite.

"The K stands for the Cretaceous and the T stands for Tertiary geologic periods. This interval of abrupt change in the Earth's history closed the Cretaceous (K) period and opened the

143

Tertiary (T) period," Clark replied.

Rick rolled his eyes. "Of course, everyone knows that," he stated flatly.

Dr. Lane, who had been listening from a short distance, glanced at Anna and Christian and then interjected, "As you are discussing this subject, let me remind you that dinosaurs are still alive and have successfully evolved into birds. They are direct descendants of the small meat-eating dinosaurs. In modern biological classification they are considered to be a subset of the Dinosauria with perhaps 8,000 species alive today."

Christian and Anna surmised that Dr. Lane meant this statement to apply more to them, than the other listeners.

"Yes, sir, but that aside, we are specifically referring to the dinosaur giants," Clark replied.

Christian was irritated, by the ridiculous remark that birds descended from dinosaurs. Realizing that Romans 1:22 said, *Claiming to be wise, they became fools*, he could be silent no longer. "Dr. Lane, if this is true, and you hold to Neo-Darwinian evolution and the survival of the fittest, how do you explain that birds have outlasted dinosaurs?"

"Yeah, most dinosaurs were huge creatures!" Anna then questioned, "You mean to say they died out while little delicate birds, are still alive? How are they superior?"

"Numerically superior of course!" Dr. Lane looked at Christian and Anna in surprise at the insight of their questions. *These misguided students actually show intelligence!*

"I agree with my brother that dinosaurs evolved into birds," Rick stated, eager to remind everyone present of his status as brother-of-the-boss. He unzipped his ever-present waistpack and pulled out some gum. "Gum anyone?"

Christian shook his head and continued speaking. "Dinosaurs are considered by most to be cold-blooded, while birds are warm-blooded. It's a big leap of faith to believe that they evolved that much."

No one commented. Dr. Lane broke the silence.

"Well, carry on and explain more to our young friends about the iridium layer that has been found." Dr. Lane glanced at his watch gauging the time. "I'm going to head to the dig. See you shortly?" he asked, more as a statement than a question.

Hearing this, Rick rose too, following his brother without glancing back.

"Yes, sir." Those not directly involved in the discussion hastily finished their breakfast to join their boss. Not many paleontologists worked full time on digs. Dr. Lane was one of perhaps thirty worldwide with this privilege, a fact the university prized.

"I still hold to the theory of the catastrophe being caused by a meteor or asteroid." Simon agreed, "which would mean an asteroid impacted what is now Mexico's Yucatan Peninsula. The main force of this impact would send a firestorm over North America. This subsequent fireball and the darkness caused severe environmental consequences, leading to the global extinction of many plants and animals, including the dinosaurs. The evidence has grown so overwhelming that few scientists dispute that an asteroid nearly six miles wide slammed into the Yucatán Coastline."

The discussion became more heated. Christian listened to the exchange as he ate a second helping of eggs and bacon.

"Didn't the asteroid theory begin sometime in 1980 and wasn't it discounted at the time?" Christian asked.

"It wasn't so much discounted as shelved for the time being. This was just one of many proposals for the extinction of the large dinosaur species," Simon qualified.

An old truck pulled up and Luke alighted just in time to hear the discussion. "Ah, the asteroid dinosaur extinction theory number 2025," he smiled walking up to pour himself a cup of coffee. He took the empty seat recently vacated by another staff member who had joined Dr. Lane at the dig.

Clark scowled at Luke, not happy to see that the Murphys might have some help in their creationist beliefs. Clark stated, "While this may be another extinction theory, as you say, it is still worth mentioning. Around 1990, the formation of fractured rocks was discovered at the northern end of the Yucatan Peninsula. The geologic formation were named Chicxulub after a nearby village. The roughly circular area is one hundred miles in diameter. The crater is buried about one kilometer below ground, half on land and half below the sea floor. Samples were taken by an oil-drilling operation. They were age-dated by scientists, with the argon-argon method, and reported to be about sixty-five million years old."

"Bingo!" Simon smiled. "The bolide, the generic name for a large asteroid from space, impacted the earth about the time frame most currently associated with the demise of the dinosaurs."

"So, this asteroid is credited with the beginning of the catastrophe which caused the extinction of dinosaurs," Christian thoughtfully munched on a piece of bacon.

"Yes. Furthermore, the iridium, which is a heavy metal element found more abundantly in meteorites, asteroids, and comets than on earth, was found in great concentration and later dispersed around the world," Simon stated bluntly.

Luke, who had been listening all this time without comment, added, "I read that in Montana, which as you know is rich in fossils, the iridium layer is two to three meters above the highest *in situ* dinosaur remains."

"Awesome, you mean *in situ* as in the original position of where the dinosaur remains were found?" Christian asked.

"Yes. That means the dinosaurs probably disappeared before any collision that may have laid down iridium," Luke said.

"Some geographic areas remain a puzzle," Simon said, frowning at Luke. "Yet it remains that the crater exists, and we believe it was the result of an asteroid that caused the extinction."

"It seems that both sides believe some catastrophic event killed the dinosaurs—the asteroid strike is a catastrophic event with a vengeance!" Christian exclaimed.

"Yes, and Pete is encased in sedimentary rock, rock laid down by running water, like a Flood. The earth is made up of seventy-two percent water with oceans that are over two and a half miles deep on average." Anna added.

"But I'm puzzled," Christian frowned, "if an asteroid caused a catastrophic event, as you say, why were the dinosaurs

146

singled out for extinction? Other mobile creatures such as tortoises, snakes, mammals, birds and fish still are alive today."

"Well, many species of animals became extinct at that time," Simon responded, coughing gently into his napkin, "and, um, some of the species, which you've mentioned, survived."

"But I thought not all dinosaurs died out at the same time," Anna asked puzzled.

"While the fossil record does show a time frame between some species' extinction, we do know that these are theories for which we are still searching for the answer," Clark said.

"We do know that iridium also comes from volcanic processes, and igneous material includes traces of iridium, especially when derived from the deep-mantle area." Luke replied, "So, it seems not all iridium would need to be attributed to an asteroid."

"Yes, you are correct," Clark said. "In fact some experts attribute dinosaur death to climatic events related to a massive outpouring of lava in India during a similar relative time in history. This area in western India is called the Deccan Traps."

"Evolutionary explanation number 2026," Luke responded evenly, not ready to let go of the debate.

"You're still holding on to your Flood theory?" asked Simon.

"Don't get him started," Clark said, groaning.

"Yes, I believe the world-wide Flood as recorded in Genesis really took place." Seeing that he still had the group's attention, he continued. "I believe the dinosaurs died out after the Flood. Some may have drowned or suffered from the cataclysmic events taking place at the time of the Flood. Such as, when a portion of the Earth's crust cracked and the subterranean aquifers, known as the fountains of the deep, were released," Luke explained. "I believe that there could have been an atmospheric vapor canopy surrounding the Earth, creating an effect similar to a hyperbaric chamber of sorts, which may have permitted temperate climates throughout the world. This canopy ceased at the time of the Flood. The ensuing rain, with possible volcanic activity, may have caused the splitting of the single super-continent. There was a 'continental sprint,' instead of a continental drift. In addition, huge tidal

147

surges redistributed sediments in layers globally."

Christian added, "And this sedimentation was laid down in a relatively brief time frame. It formed most of the geologic column but not in the time frame given by evolutionists. This would easily explain why some sections of the column are missing in some geographic areas, such as the Grand Canyon."

Simon was floored by what he had heard. "Let's not get into the geologic column right now. Let's stick to this Flood story. I can't imagine anyone buying into that fairy tale."

"A fairy tale is a frog turning into a prince, or a dinosaur turning into a bird, given a few million years," Anna replied sweetly.

The men laughed in spite of themselves. Simon tried to hide a smile and said, "But, Anna, what we believe is based on scientific facts."

"From what I understand of the Flood, it makes more sense that the juvenile dinosaurs, leaving the Ark would find a different world with many climate changes, than they did upon boarding. They would die out at different times, due to an inadequate food supply, after the flooding or other events that took place," Christian responded.

"I believe it took millions of years for each of the layers to be laid down and for them to harden," Clark said. "And you believe these sedimentary layers were laid down by the flood and not over each other as I do."

"Yes, we believe the sedimentation occurred rapidly. As the Flood waters rushed into new low-lying areas carrying much of the soft, wet terrain with it as the waters drained into the sea. Many creatures were washed away with the receding waters, such as our friend the dinosaur. Many were rapidly buried in sedimentary layers and have hardened fairly fast, within years at most, not millions, of years." Luke said. "Even the acids or bases in the soil will eat at the bones without the right conditions."

"I still agree with Clark. I don't believe fossilization could occur in such a short span of time," Simon stated.

"Well, here is a scientific fact for you. There is a large area in Australia where fossilized jellyfish have been found. Even

148

jellyfish didn't have time to decay or be eaten by scavengers. It took rapid burying of sediment to cause this to happen, like that from the Flood." Luke said

"Floods form fossils fast!" Christian said.

"I think you are forgetting the most current findings," Luke stated. "My own research has shown that if a bone is not buried or underwater within one-to-two years of de-fleshing, it will literally deteriorate. Do you agree?"

Both men nodded their heads as Anna and Christian listened with interest.

"In fact, a bone must be buried to become a fossil. If a bone is buried or underwater, a process of chemical and physical change begins turning it into a fossil. A bone can be completely converted into a mineral substance, which becomes fossilized within a few years. In some special environments, such as the volcano eruption at Mt. St. Helens, fossilization occurred within a few months. The main requirement is rapid burial, or submergence."

"I hate to say this," Simon said looking at Clark, "but I read a similar paper on rapid fossilization recently on the Internet. And, the particular website held to evolutionary beliefs."

"What?" Clark said, incredulously. He quickly recovered, "Well, like I said, there are many mysteries surrounding dinosaur extinction. But one thing that is not a mystery is that we'll all be replaced, by Dr. Lane, if we don't hightail it down to the dig site now," Simon grabbed his paper plate and coffee cup as he nodded to the group. Everyone rose, except for Luke and the Murphys.

"Well, I guess you told them," Anna responded smiling, as she began to clear away traces of their meal.

"Yes," Luke sighed rubbing his brow, "It's incredible that I even got this position; because, I'm not an evolutionist. I think my long standing friendship with the university's president is the only reason I'm tolerated around here."

"Can you believe all the conjecture? It's amazing how scientists will use any other reason, except a global Flood, to account for extinction," Christian said.

"What puzzles me is the excuses given for missing layers of the geologic column," Anna said. "It's pushed aside as a non-question."

"When you don't have an answer, the question is considered unimportant." Luke agreed. "What most people don't realize is the geologic column was age-dated long before radioactive methods were invented. The surprising truth is the ages those old-time scientists gave the rocks are considered more accurate than the much more scientific dating methods used today."

"I think the evidence continues to point to a young Earth," Christian said. "I've been meaning to ask you, Dr. Lane mentioned finding an index fossil, the tuatara which he is using to age-date Pete. I was going to research it."

"Don't bother, it's not extinct." Luke smiled, "It's a living fossil. It's been found alive in New Zealand."

"Ha! That's great." Christian said smiling.

"And does Dr. Lane know this?" Anna asked.

"Yes, but he still is using it as an index fossil and says it proves Pete is 65-million years old. But, I may have a breakthrough to share with you soon. I'm praying for the Lord's timing in bringing it to light..." Luke trailed off.

"You got the results from the university on the bone fragments!" Christian guessed.

"Not all of them." Luke said.

"Well? Are they truly bone that hasn't gone through fossilization?" Christian persisted.

"It's more than that. We may have found some blood vessel channels." Luke added, "It will shake the belief of many scientists on this dig."

"Can't you tell us any more?" Christian asked.

"Not right now, but be praying. We can use all the prayers we can get." Luke rose from the table.

"Are you coming down to the dig?" Anna asked, dying to know what Luke meant but not wanting to pry further.

"No, most of my time today is going to be spent here in our makeshift lab. I'm trying to patiently wait until the lab staff at the university either confirms or rejects my suspicions. I'm waiting to get a report back any day now." Luke offered, "Would you like me to help you rappel down?"

* * * * * * * *

Later that morning Anna was happy to see Christian working alongside Dr. Lane. They seemed to be getting along fairly well, and she knew her brother enjoyed the opportunity to dig as much as she was enjoying her photography. The view was beyond words. Sedimentary rock rose up in all directions. Longs Peak was the highest point of Rocky Mountain National Park. Anna literally felt like she was standing on the edge of another world. Here in the mountains, she could view God's creation from a different perspective. It was difficult to concentrate solely on the dig, as awesome as that was to her. She also took her time to photograph the surrounding scenery.

Anna walked over to a water cooler, filling her bottle. Christian soon joined her frowning.

"That man is trying his hardest to convert me," Christian said, gesturing toward Dr. Lane.

"You're making it sound as if evolution was a pagan religion," Anna laughed.

"His version is! To hear him tell it, creation is at odds with anything scientific." Christian huffed.

"I can't believe the man is convinced that evolution has been proven, and transitions are all over the place." Anna sighed.

"Remember Anna, 2 Timothy 4:3 says, 'For the time is coming when people will not endure sound teaching, . . .they will accumulate for themselves teachers to suit their own likings, and will turn away from listening to the truth and wander into myths.'"

Just then a whoop was heard among the workers. Christian and Anna had been so deep in conversation that they didn't notice Luke had descended to the dig. They walked over to the staff making a semicircle facing Luke. Dr. Lane was scowling as he asked Luke a question. They were just in time to hear his words.

"Yes, you heard me right. We have found red blood cells

151

in the section of bone we excavated, the piece that broke turned out to be unfossilized deep within. We took a sliver and examined it here, and then I sent a portion of bone to the lab at the university and asked them to examine it. They agree."

A hush fell over the crowd as they took in the implication.

"But that's impossible!" Dr. Lane could barely keep his composure. "There is no way that could happen. Red blood cells could not have lasted 65 million years!"

"But, we have the evidence. And what the evidence means is that this dinosaur is not millions of years old," Luke said.

Chapter 20
The Anomaly

General panic broke out as everyone began speaking at once. Luke was bombarded with questions, all being fired in rapid succession. He tried to field them as best he could and was finally glad to hear Dr. Lane's authoritative voice break in above the mayhem.

"Please, gentlemen, there is no need for alarm; obviously the results are incorrect."

"What exactly did you find?" Rick asked in annoyance. He reached down to unzip his waistpack and gasped . . . it wasn't there. "Hey! Has anyone seen my waistpack?"

"Now is not the time for lost and found," Dr. Lane said, abruptly silencing his brother.

"Start at the beginning," Christian asked. "Are you talking about the bone that broke when we were here?"

Rick looked at him in anger, "This really isn't any of your business; but, if you must know, yes. Someone, who we all know," he glared at Luke, "didn't prepare the leg bone well enough for transportation up the mountain."

"Dropping it from a height of thirty feet didn't help the situation," Luke responded, not willing to take all of the blame.

"Be that as it may," Dr. Lane took over, "the bone broke in half, but the damage could be easily repaired."

"That was my job to repair the bone," Luke said. "But, Christian first noticed something strange in the cross section. When I looked, I found that some portions of the leg, deep within, were not fossilized. At first, I couldn't believe it. Then, upon further examination, I took a thin section of the bone and looked at it under a microscope."

"What did you see?" Simon asked in a hushed tone.

"At first just bone that wasn't fossilized," Luke said. "Then, upon closer inspection with another specimen from the bone, I found blood vessel channels."

"So?" Rick said.

"But, that's not all," Luke responded, pausing for effect, "I looked closer and saw tiny round objects, translucent red with a dark center. They could only be red blood cells."

Once again, everyone began talking and firing questions one after another.

"Why didn't you tell us?" Simon asked.

"I thought it better to get some other opinions first. I was sure, not everyone would agree with my interpretation, of what I saw," Luke explained.

"Who has substantiated your results in the lab?" Clark asked.

"Dr. Larson and Dr. Peters," Luke answered.

"Have you seen the results, Dr. Lane?" Clark asked in dismay. Larson and Peters were highly regarded members of the university staff, yet he was hoping Dr. Lane would put an end to this madness.

"No, I didn't see the specimen that was sent to the university lab." There was a murmur of approval, which quickly died down with the next sentence.

"But, I did see the specimen in our lab up top," Dr. Lane sighed. "There is only one solution."

"Which is?" Luke's mouth tightened, for he suspected what Dr. Lane might say.

"Just prove that they really aren't red blood cells," Dr. Lane said. His steely bespectacled gaze would have caused a lesser man to back down.

Luke gazed back with the same conviction. "I did that, sir, as you ordered me to do, a few days ago. That is why I sent a specimen to the lab. Their findings substantiated my own."

Once again the crowd vied to be heard as they asked question after question. Christian tugged on Anna's arm. Once he had gotten her attention, he motioned with his head toward the dinosaur bones, which were all but forgotten with this new bit of news.

Christian pulled his sister aside and leaned over to whisper, "I guess the Earth is not as old as they think."

"Why bother to whisper? I don't think they'd hear a bomb go off!" Anna said, astounded that such highly trained scientists could get so worked up over tiny blood cells.

"You're right," Christian grinned; "They know the fossil cannot possibly be millions of years old if blood cells have been found. They just can't believe it. Isn't this great!"

Anna smiled at her brother's enthusiasm. Then she photographed the group gathered around Luke. "This will definitely be a moment to remember," she agreed.

"I guess this shouldn't be a surprise to us. It certainly fits into the creation model," Christian mused aloud.

"I'm going to stay here and take some pictures since there is no one blocking my view," Anna said.

"Okay, I'm going back to hear poor Luke get questioned to death." Christian walked back to the group.

"So, what now? Are they going to search for DNA?" Clark asked.

"No, while that is a tempting prospect. As you know, we find DNA in every living organism... from fungi, to bacteria, to our fingerprints. It's too hard to be sure that the DNA came from the specimen," Luke explained.

"What exactly was tested in the lab?" Simon asked,

brushing off his sleeves. He had been excavating earlier, and his clothes were covered with a layer of dust.

"Well, the tissue was a reddish-brown color, as was the liquid which was extracted from the dinosaur tissue. As you know, hemoglobin is that color."

"And," Simon cut Luke off impatiently, "what else?"

"Various other tests were run to prove that it was indeed hemoglobin," Luke replied.

"Well, hemoglobin contains heme units. Were tests done to prove the heme units exist?" Clark asked.

"What are heme units?" Christian asked.

"They are the deep red, non-protein, iron component of blood," Dr. Lane responded, "Well? Was the laser test run?"

"Yes, chemical signatures unique to heme were found in the specimens when certain wavelengths of laser light were applied," Luke sighed. "and, because it contains iron, heme reacts to magnetic fields differently than other proteins. Extracts from our specimen reacted in the same way as modern heme compounds."

"And the rat test?" Dr. Lane asked, knowing that a test had been conducted where a tiny extract of the dinosaur specimen had been injected into rats. If there were even a minute amount of hemoglobin present in the *T. rex* sample, the immune system of the rats would build up antibodies against the compound.

"It's not definite; it's too soon to tell. The rat's immune system did build up some antibodies, but the tests will take another ten days to be sure," Luke said. A hush could be heard as everyone contemplated the news.

Several seconds passed before Dr. Lane spoke, "I'm going back to the university. I'm going to extract my own specimen since the leg bone has been transported there. And, I'm going to oversee my own tests, especially the rat experimentation. I just can't believe the specimen contains red blood cells. Luke, take over until I return."

Chapter 21
Another Incident

The sun had begun its downward descent earlier. Now at five-thirty, the fluffy clouds were turning a warm orange, which contrasted the cooling temperatures. Two hours earlier, Dr. Lane had returned to the university, as promised. Now, the dig site was completely quiet, except for an occasional comment from Anna or Christian. Everyone else had left at 5:00pm sharp. The snap of Anna's camera was the only other sound to be heard.

"I only need a few more pictures," Anna stated as she snapped away at the skull. "Christian, can you move the tripod a little to the right?" More of the *T. rex* teeth Christian found the other day, had been exposed and she wanted another shot.

"Sure," he quickly scooted it a few feet, adjusting the legs to hold the tripod steady.

Anna attached a 100 mm macro lens onto her 35 mm camera.

"How's that?" he questioned.

"Just perfect."

With Dr. Lane gone, Luke had little choice but to stay and make sure everything had been secured for the night, which was usually Dr. Lane's job.

Anna saw Luke approaching and said, "I'm glad you didn't mind us staying late; this is exactly the angle I was looking for." She rummaged around in her backpack looking for more film. "Its also nice not to worry about people being in the way."

"No problem. I'm glad it worked out. I had to stay late anyway," Luke answered as he walked up.

Anna nodded her thanks. As it turned out, Luke had wanted everything in proper order. He had been finishing up his notes for the past hour while the Murphys took pictures.

"Christian, please come here for a second; I need you to move that pick," Anna said, pointing to a rock pile.

"As soon as you're through, we can head up together," Luke said. "No need to hurry, though."

Now able to relax, Luke waited for the Murphys to finish up. He stood back, his hands stuffed into his jean pockets, as he leisurely leaned against a rock and silently watched the Murphys. He admired the way Christian and Anna worked as a team.

About ten minutes later, Anna announced, "That'll do it. I say we're finished," she said with a sense of accomplishment.

"About time," Christian said teasingly as he helped Anna pack. "I was about ready to unroll my sleeping bag for the night."

"The way you've been acting," Anna stated with a fake solemn expression, "I thought a few times you were already sleeping."

Christian grinned at her. " Nah, I always act like that."

"For once, Christian, I totally and completely agree with you!" Anna tried unsuccessfully to keep a straight face as they continued their playful teasing.

She expertly dismantled the camera from the tripod and began to fold everything down. Within minutes, all the equipment was stored in their backpacks.

Meanwhile, Luke's thoughts turned from the teens to his ever-present worry of the dig. Actually it wasn't so much the dig, but his worry of Troy. *What kind of damage to creation science*

158

could he have accomplished if the Lord had not put me here to preserve this amazing find? He wondered. *If only I could figure out a way to make Troy understand! I want so much for him to comprehend the creation perspective. This would certainly help not only the scientific world, but also in Troy's personal life, too.*

Hearing the Murphy's banter, Luke looked up at them, smiling. *I wonder if Anna and Christian realize how much headway they have made with Troy?* Luke knew that Troy had once thought that the Murphys would be easy converts. However, Troy had switched from the offensive to the defensive angle when they were around. He had little opportunity to trip them up or discredit their faith like he was so used to doing. *I'm so glad. These two kids just might be the best thing that could happen to Troy. God can do great things with and through people who are open to Him,* Luke nodded to himself. He knew from personal experience how the wonders of creation were a testament of His love, if only Troy would open his heart to God's leading.

"Luke?" Anna said for the second time, waiting for a response. When she got no answer she tried a third time. "Luke? We're just about done packing up." Anna's last words brought him abruptly out of his thoughts.

"Oh, what was that?" Luke's brow was furrowed.

" Did I interrupt something?" Anna asked apologetically.

"Oh no, I mean . . ." Luke trailed off sheepishly. "I was just trying to solve the world's problems."

"Have any luck?" Christian asked as he walked up from behind his sister.

"Nope," Luke grinned and continued. "I was actually trying to think of a way to convince Troy that he needs Jesus in his life. With creation science, I was hoping to lead him to the light, however, unlikely that proposition would sound to Troy."

"Anything is possible with Jesus behind you," Anna said with conviction.

"That's what I was thinking! All I need to do is pray for him and be patient." Luke's voice lost its seriousness and filled with humor as he said, "No doubt about it, I'll be a saint for sure by the time this excavation is completed."

159

Thirty minutes later they had all scaled the mountain, this time without any mishap. Dr. Lane had ordered that all ropes be thoroughly checked before being lowered. The climbing equipment had been deposited, in a supply tent, before they made their way to the car, flashlight in hand. Simon had headed to his tent as soon as they reached the gravel driveway where the vehicles had been parked earlier that morning.

Without the whine of the generator, which powered the rope pulley and floodlights, the mountain had a quiet eeriness. The three watched their flashlight beams bounce along the path.

"It's really d— " Christian stopped short as he tripped over a protruding root. Thump!

"Man! My toe." Christian hopped up and down holding his foot in pain.

Luke was about to reply when he stopped walking. "What's that hissing?" Luke asked as the other two came to a halt fifteen feet from the vehicles.

Anna shrugged, looking down at her feet. "It's too cold for a snake to be moving around, isn't it?" she asked with concern.

Christian's hurt foot was forgotten as he said, "Hmm . . . I don't think it's a snake. Though we're in the wrong climate for this, I once saw a program where the people thought they had a flat tire because they heard hissing. They even called a tow truck. It turned out to be an alligator under the car!"

"Hey, that could be it!" Before Anna or Christian could make a comment he continued, "Not an alligator, but a flat tire." Luke groaned. "Just what I needed."

"I hope it's not the Hummer. I don't want to have to explain this one to the Sullivans," Christian said with a frown.

"I doubt they'd care," Anna said.

"Well, I've got good news and bad news. The good news is, Christian, you won't have to explain this to anyone. The bad news is, I'll need a lift home." Luke bent down. His flashlight revealed a deflated tire. Further inspection revealed that all four tires were out of air.

"How do you like that?" Luke asked Christian.

160

"Yeah, it looks like someone stuck a toothpick into the core and broke it off," Christian confirmed Luke's suspicions.

"Who would have done such a thing?" Anna asked with a shudder.

Running a hand through his hair Luke said, "I just don't know . . . for sure."

"Hmm . . . you don't think Simon would be playing a joke, do you?" Christian asked.

"Some joke," Luke said in dismay, dismissing it with a shake of his head. "No, that doesn't make sense. Someone wouldn't do this as a joke; and, if they were trying to hurt me, then it couldn't be Simon. He's the first one we would suspect."

Christian walked around the truck, flashlight in hand, using the beam to sweep the area.

"What are you doing?" Anna asked.

"Looking for a buttercup. Nope, none here."

"Are you going to call the police?" Anna asked Luke.

"Yes, when I get home," Luke answered.

"Got any enemies?" Christian asked.

He took the question as a joke and dismissed the remark, but Christian was only partly teasing. Luke opened the passenger door and gasped, "Look at this." He held up a delicate yellow buttercup.

"I guess we have our answer— Lawrence Edelman!" Christian said in disgust.

I can't believe there have been two incidents here in less than one week! Christian thought. *This one looks intentional, and the rope being severed was too.* He didn't want to reveal his fears to anyone, not yet anyway. "Hop in, we'll give you a lift home," he said, out loud to Luke once he had collected his belongings.

Anna slipped into the back seat and shut the door. She deposited her backpack on the floor and rubbed her hands together attempting to warm them.

The engine roared. "Please turn on some heat, I'm freezing!" Anna said from the back.

Christian, nearly as cold as Anna, readily complied.

The majority of the trip to Luke's house was spent talking about Lawrence.

"Why couldn't anyone find him? I mean, what about experienced Park rangers?" Don't they know every inch of the Park?" Anna asked Luke.

"This park has more than 350 miles of trail. There are many backcountry paths that are difficult to find," Luke said. "Besides, many have tried to find Lawrence with no success. Believe it or not, Rick is about as experienced as Park rangers get and has spent days out in the backwoods, looking for Lawrence, but came back empty handed."

Twenty-five minutes later, Christian pulled the Hummer up in front of a one-story, brick house. "Thanks for the lift," Luke said. "Why don't you come in and meet my wife and son?"

Christian was about to decline, but knowing his sister, she'd want to see the baby. "Just for a minute. Then we need to get back," he said.

"Thanks, Christian," Anna whispered.

Christian nodded and smiled.

Luke pushed open the door. "Kate, I'm home. I've brought someone to meet you!"

A smiling petite woman in her mid-twenties came into the living room to greet them. She carried their eleven-month old baby on her hip. The woman had blond, shoulder-length hair, and large green eyes.

The blue-eyed, bald headed baby wiggled his feet and giggled when he spotted his Daddy. Luke took the child, and swung him around, as they both laughed.

Once all the introductions were made, Anna asked to hold the baby. He was a few months older than the Murphy twins and so cute, to Anna anyway. She really missed her brothers and sister.

Luke quickly told Kate about what had happened.

"I just knew it! It's got to be that man!" she stated with conviction.

"Kate, please. We don't know who did it." Luke tried unsuccessfully to quiet his wife.

"Luke, you are too nice. It just has to be either Troy or his brother . . . I can't remember his name."

"Oh, you must mean Rick?" Christian asked.

"Yes, that's exactly who I'm talking about. He was next in line for Luke's job, when Lewis became ill. Poor man," Kate said with sympathy. "The elderly gentleman, I feel so badly for him. He was such a sweet man."

"What happened to him?" Anna asked as she happily bounced the baby.

Luke answered for his wife. "He quit before I came here, but we met him a few times. He claims that he was poisoned, but the police could never find any evidence to prove it. He had accidents in the Park. They were all blamed on Lawrence. He does, after all, leave a buttercup."

"Anyway," Kate continued, "Rick thought he was going to get the job, his brother being in charge and all. Besides, he works at the Park and spends every spare weekend and free time on the dig."

Luke took up the story as the baby began to fuss. "But then, I messed up his plans. I applied for the position, and among other things, the paleontology department at the university liked the fact that I was also a professor," Luke shrugged. "So, they picked me instead."

"That could be a good enough reason for Rick to try and get revenge," Christian said, agreeing with Kate.

"But, it doesn't really make sense. Besides, we don't want to falsely accuse anyone," Luke said. "I can't believe anyone would be that ruthless, just for a job position."

Kate nodded, but didn't say anything.

"The two most recent unexplainable incidents at the park are the rope breaking and my tires being deflated. The first happened to Christian, not me. If Rick was the cause, why would Rick try to hurt Christian?" No one answered.

Anna suddenly remembered something she didn't respond to at the time. *Dr. Lane had been angry. And, he had shouted that Luke was supposed to climb up first. Was Rick really the culprit? Had he intentionally cut the rope, which he thought was going to be climbed by Luke? If so, why?*

Luke went on, "And the second incident was my tires. That prank wouldn't make me stop working on the dig so it would be fruitless for Rick or Troy to do it. Besides, Troy had already returned to the university. And the first mishap was previously blamed on Lawrence. The second mishap also will be blamed on Lawrence, after I tell the police about the flower."

Anna and Christian both listened to the explanation with mixed emotions. They were still wondering if Kate was right, however, unlikely Luke made it sound. Besides, they reasoned with themselves, Luke had no reason to defend Rick unless he was sure Rick had nothing to do with it. Luke had simply stated the facts. In this case they spoke louder than personal differences or dislikes.

Chapter 22
Not Lost, Found

Early Sunday afternoon the teens Christian, Anna, Scott, and Kayla gathered together again. They planned a day of hiking that started at Glacier Gorge junction trailhead, which was northwest of Diamond Peak. Anna and Christian had spent the morning after church readying a package to mail to their father. It contained developed photos of the dig, along with a letter and a small present for their brother. Although they had been sending e-mails to Andy, they knew he would appreciate something personal.

In contrast to the day they spent in town shopping, Kayla was out of her element.

"I can't believe I let you talk me into coming on this hike," Kayla said as she gingerly picked her way a long the trail beside Anna. "I've already broken a nail!"

Anna lowered her camera and smiled. She wasn't sure if Kayla was serious or not and was about to offer her sympathy.

Kayla cut her off before she could begin. Holding up her hand in protest, she said, "I know it's only fair; after all you did come shopping with me."

Anna smiled. "You really will enjoy hiking. I promise! Just give it a chance," she suggested. "The spectacular view will be worth the effort!"

Scott and Christian walked a few feet ahead of Anna and Kayla, deep in conversation. Scott sported a khaki vest and back-pack overflowing with gadgets. He had binoculars with a 52x zoom capability, the world's most powerful civilian engineered. Another one of his Dad's inventions, that Scott carried, was an advanced night scope with a built-in movie camera feature. Scott thought of almost everything, from MRE food rations to a sur-vival kit and water.

The four hiked heading due west along the approximately two-mile trail to Flattop Mountain. There they would rest; Anna would take some pictures, and then they would head back.

They had been hiking for about thirty minutes when Kayla announced that she needed a break. Sitting down on a fallen log, Kayla cringed at her new clothes. She had purchased them for the trip; everything down to the best hiking scarf money could buy. She reached down to brush off her supple leather boots and loosen the too-tight laces. Then she brushed her pants. "I've never been so dirty in my entire life!"

Laughingly, Anna related a story to Kayla about when they had been in Arcadia, Florida. "You should have seen us! We were covered in sand and mud from head-to-toe and soaking wet from a rainstorm! Christian can attest to that!"

Kayla looked incredulous, "You're kidding, right?"

Christian shook his head smiling. "We were on an ar-chaeological excavation along the Peace River. It started to rain and, well, you can figure out what happened from there."

"Actually, I can imagine," Kayla said, smiling. Even though she had little in common with Anna and Christian, their sincerity was appealing. There was nothing pretentious about those two.

"You know, I've been doing some research on my own," Scott said, seated on a sloping bolder, overlooking the view of the mountains in the distance.

"What kind of research?" Christian asked, eager to hear about another invention.

"Creation science research," Scott said.

"You should see his room. He's already printed enough information to write his own book," Kayla said, "and if that isn't bad enough, he wants to tell me all he has learned."

"Really?" Christian said, with interest, "so, what have you learned?"

"I think you may be onto something. You know, I always took evolutionary beliefs at face value because we were taught it as fact in school. I reconciled these beliefs to my church's teachings easily. As long as I believed God created the world, I thought that was the end of the discussion. But truthfully?" Scott raked his hands through his short straight hair. "I was having a more and more difficult time reconciling the two views. When we had that conversation at lunch I really started to question it all. I found some awesome web sites and some of them offer online classes."

"He's already signed up and with our Dad's blessing! I think Dad is glad that Scott is continuing his education, no matter what it is," Kayla said, stretching out and wiggling her legs and booted feet. "You know, these are kind of cute; I wonder if you could get them in other colors, like crimson?"

Anna and Christian grinned, and then dissolved into laughter at Kayla's comment. "Red hiking boots would definitely be different," Anna said. Still smiling, she then turned to Scott, "I'm so very glad you are seriously studying creation science."

"Well, I already know the evolutionary side of science, so I thought I might as well get some balance," Scott agreed, "I'm fascinated with everything I've read. It makes so much sense to me now. I showed the information to my Dad, and well, we're talking again—something we haven't done in a long time. He really was interested in finding out more and agreed to let me study the subject online."

"Many very good creation scientists once believed evolution wholeheartedly. A number even hold advanced science degrees from secular universities. Who knows, some day you may be one of the 'greats'!" Christian said, enthusiastically.

"Stranger things have happened," Scott grinned.

By mutual consent they stood and continued on the trail. Scott took the lead, heading toward thick vegetation.

"Scott, the trail goes this way, even I can see that!" Kayla announced to the retreating back of her brother and Christian several feet ahead.

Turning around, Scott stopped and proudly held up a wristwatch device as if that was explanation enough. "We've got this. We can't get lost!"

"Another two-way radio?" Anna asked, remembering the one she had used in town days before.

Shaking his head, Scott said, "Actually, it's a GPS. Which stands for . . ."

"Global positioning satellite," Kayla said, stomping her foot with feigning impatience.

Anna exchanged looks with Christian. She secretly thought Kayla was much prouder of her brother and father than she ever let on. "I've heard of a GPS. I guess for some reason I've always thought they were bigger."

"As you might have guessed, this one is even better," Christian answered his sister. Mr. Song Le is getting the wristwatch design patent, and he's hoping the military will use it in the future."

"He's right," Scott stated smiling, "a larger version of it was developed for military use. Dad and I took the technology and made it smaller and more advanced."

"What can it do and exactly how does it work?"

Scott needed little encouragement to talk about his inventions, "This one can display data to help in unfamiliar territory. It will track your current position and map the distance you've gone. And the tracking screen will even show your progress with a blinking cursor. The GPS technology works by picking up the signals of twenty-seven satellites orbiting the Earth to keep you from getting lost. Perfect for out here," Scott gestured to the sharp peaks and steep trail in front of them. "You just can't get lost with one of these."

168

"Thank you for the geography lesson, 'mon frere,' " Kayla stated, hiding a smile and translating, "that means my brother."

"Scott and I want to try it out," Christian announced. "We're going to forge our own trail to Flattop Mountain, maybe turn a three-mile hike into two."

"I'd love to see how it works," Anna said.

Kayla looked uncertain; "Well, if it will be quicker. But, do you really think it's a good idea to actually *try* to get lost?" Kayla didn't bother to ask her brother. She knew how he'd answer, but looked pleadingly at Anna and Christian, afraid she was outnumbered.

"We're not trying to get lost. We're just saying that if we get lost, there is help. It's safe, and of course, it has been tested." Scott answered. "Come on, Kayla."

Not wanting to spoil the trip for the rest of them, Kayla squared her shoulders and stepped off the trail. To everyone's relief, this effectively ended the discussion. Soon they formed in a single file line, forging a new trail with the GPS as a guide.

Hiking along for over thirty minutes, they trekked through a dense population of lodgepole pines. The group came across several clearings that, they quickly surmised, backpackers had used for campsites. They were amazed, however, to find little in the way of debris.

Anna stopped a few minutes later and peered around. "Check it out."

"What?" Christian asked.

"I think we're standing in the middle of a campsite!" Anna exclaimed, pointing around her. "See what I mean?"

"Wow, you're right! I almost missed it! This is weird. Someone obviously doesn't want anyone to know they're here," Scott answered, pointing to the cleverly hidden camouflage tent under a pine tree and brush.

Kayla smiled, readjusting her chic sombrero hat, which was especially purchased for the occasion. "Let's be neighborly," she said brightly.

There wasn't much of a clearing; the two-man tent barely fit between two towering trees and was expertly concealed with leaves and branches. Only upon closer inspection was the camp-site distinguishable. The remains of a little fire pit were barely visible as it was covered with dirt and branches.

"Hello? Anybody home?" Kayla called. The quiet rustling of the forest was all that replied. "They must be out," she finally concluded.

"Were you expecting to recognize them, Kayla? This isn't the local country club, you know." Scott teased.

"You never know! Let's have a look around while they're out."

Scott, with Kayla in tow, walked over to the tent and called, "Anybody home?" No one answered and so Scott unzipped the flap.

Anna and Christian were taken aback. They didn't like snooping around in other people belongings. "I'm not sure you should go in," Christian warned them both.

"Oh, come on. No one's here," Scott chided.

Christian shrugged in disapproval but said no more to Scott. Turning to Anna, he said, "Check this place out; it's bizarre!"

"I know what you mean. It's as though someone is hiding something," Anna agreed in a hushed tone. The area seemed shrouded in mystery.

Meanwhile, Scott had ducked inside the tent. "No one's home," he said to Kayla who was peeking inside.

Kayla pulled the flap open wider. Bending down she took inventory. "Let's see, the interior has been done in early campground with a neo-survival man flair. We have a cramped living quarter, topped off with a roll-a-way bed, okay, a sleeping bag rolled up in the corner and several backpacks sporting a camouflage design, new for fall."

Anna giggled in spite of herself. "Okay, we've seen enough; time to go."

"Who's our mysterious camper?" Kayla asked Scott, who had something in his hand.

"I don't know, but check out this flower." Scott held up a bright yellow flower for all of them to see.

170

Anna gasped.

Christian instantly knew where he had seen it before. "Be careful! That flower is poisonous!" he exclaimed then whispered in awe, "We've stumbled into Lawrence Edelman's hideout."

"Who's Lawrence?" Kayla asked in confusion.

"He's the tree hugger who's been on the news, an extreme environmentalist who's been sabotaging the whole Park in an attempt to get people to leave," said Scott. "Lawrence has been hiding up here for at least the past six months!"

"Give me a break! How do you know this is his campsite?"

"Because of his calling card; he leaves the yellow buttercup every time he sabotages something," Christian pointed to the yellow bud still in Scott's hand. "He wants to let everyone know he doesn't like what they're doing to the environment."

"I've seen . . ."

Kayla cut off Anna, "You're kidding right?" Her dark eyes flashing, silently pleading with someone to start laughing and tell her it was only a joke, but no one did.

Scott was busily going through Lawrence's belongings. Scott held up a black waistpack close enough for Christian to see. "I thought you said his name was Lawrence? This monogram says R.L."

Christian looked at the waistpack. It somehow looked familiar. As he studied the green thread stitched onto the front of the backpack, it dawned on him.

"Hey! This is Rick Lane's missing waistpack!" Christian exclaimed. "He was looking for it the other day."

Scott looked up with interest from where he had been rummaging around seconds before. "How in the world did it get here?"

"Lawrence must have stolen it!" Kayla snapped.

The others quickly agreed with Kayla's assumption. That was the only logical conclusion.

"We have to take it back to him!" Anna said with conviction.

"Won't he be surprised!" Kayla added. "He must have

been really worried."

"Yeah, we were there when he yelled about it being missing." Anna agreed.

"Let's see what's in it?" Scott made a grab for the pack.

Before Christian could protest, Scott had snatched it away and unzipped it. He let out a low whistle, "Take a look at these!" Scott held up a glistening diamond necklace. The sun played on the multifaceted gems.

"Are they real?" Anna asked

"I doubt it," Scott said.

Kayla took the necklace from Scott's outstretched hand and with a critical eye examined it. "It's real," she stated with assurance.

"No way!" Scott said scoffing. "Why would Rick have a real diamond necklace anyway, on a backwoods trail, no less."

"I don't know, but I'm sure they're real. Now let's get out of here! What if he comes back?" Kayla said, worry evident in her voice.

"I agree with Kayla," Anna confirmed. "Come on Christian and Scott. Let's take the waistpack and go."

The boys voiced their agreement as they swiftly put back the other belongings. All four hurried out of the camp as quickly as they could, leaving no traces of their presence except for the missing waistpack that was now safely inside Anna's backpack. Scott, with his GPS strapped to his wrist, wordlessly led the group away from the area.

"We've got to tell the police," Scott insisted. He quickly plotted the camp's coordinates and saved the exact location and landmarks on the GPS.

Chapter 23
Ghost of the Rockies

Uneasiness shrouded the four like a heavy, wet blanket, with a feeling of dread that they just couldn't shake. By now most of the small talk, which had accompanied them before, was abandoned. They were intent on getting out of the woods without a confrontation with Lawrence.

Forty-five minutes later they were still trudging along. Scott had taken the lead as before, the Murphys were in the middle; and Kayla lagged, bringing up the rear. Douglas firs lined the left side of the trail. On the opposite side of the trail, a sharp cliff dropped downward.

Christian took off his baseball cap, and repositioned it as he turned around, looking behind him. "I can't explain it, but I feel like someone's watching," Christian said in hushed tones.

Anna responded, "I feel the same way too, Christian."

Moments later she raised her camera, still trying to shake off her uncertainty. Stopping, she focused in and shot several pictures of a large bald eagle soaring above the trees in the bright blue sky. Kayla, with her head still down, nearly bumped into Anna.

"Oh, sorry, Anna," she apologized.

Seconds later Kayla uttered a strained gasp, "Anna!"

"Hmm?" Anna lowered her camera to see what had scared Kayla. *Has she broken another nail?*

Kayla grabbed Anna's shoulder. "Anna! There's a creature! Over to ... the ..." Her words ended in a scream.

Anna and the two boys wheeled around; Kayla was shaking with fear. An instant later, before anyone could utter a word, a tawny streak exploded from the trees to their left. Still ten feet away it sprung, landing squarely on Kayla, and knocking her to the ground.

Screeching, Kayla kicked, flailing her arms and legs in panic. She threw the startled cat off and desperately tried to get away. She crawled on her hands and knees, vainly trying to distance herself from the angry animal. It was crouched and hissing.

"Someone do something!" Anna pleaded with Christian or Scott.

Christian yelled. "We've got to get the cougar away from here," he sprinted past Anna, waving his arms.

Scott was in shock, unable to move.

"Scott, help!" Kayla screeched.

Her scream propelled Scott into action. He threw off his backpack and snatched a branch from an aspen tree. He ran yelling, headlong into the mountain lion, jabbing the animal with the branch. The cougar snarled and tried to pounce again, but this time Scott was there, holding the branch in front of him like a weapon. The angry animal pawed the stick.

Christian tried to make himself look as large as possible. He found a stick of his own and began to yell angrily and loudly as he advanced on the wild cat. He brought his foot back and kicked its side. *It's like kicking a dog!* Christian thought in desperation. *God, keep us safe! Put your hedge of protection around us,* he silently prayed.

Though Scott had stopped the cougar from attacking Kayla, the ninety-pound cat was intently eyeing its next prey.

Both boys were waving sticks and yelling, yet the animal stood its ground and bared its teeth at Christian and Scott.

Anna wanted to help, but how? She ran over to Scott's backpack and quickly dumped its contents onto the ground. *He has got to have some sort of gadget that I can use in here,* Anna thought in a panic.

A few feet away Kayla had slowly edged away from the animal. Instead of heading toward Anna, she was unknowingly heading straight for the drop-off. *Lord, please let her see it!* Anna prayed as she glanced over at Kayla for a second time.

Anna's frantic search came to an abrupt halt and she held up a small square device in triumph. "Yes! An electric stunner!"

Less than ten feet away, the mountain lion batted the stick with its paw. Tired of the noise, the animal looked around for an easier target. Without warning, the cat pounced on Kayla, digging his claws into her foot. Her supple leather boots were no match for the sharp cat's claws.

Excruciating pain shot up Kayla's leg as she cried out in agony and fell to the ground.

Scott ran at the cat letting out all his pent-up fury. He slammed the stick down right on top of the cougar's head. Releasing Kayla's foot, an enraged growl thundered from the mountain lion's massive chest. Scott backed up as he saw that the animal was now after him.

"Scott! How do I use this?" Anna yelled, running toward the animal and Scott, as she waved the stunner.

Scott diverted his gaze from the cougar to Anna. "Stop right there! Point the laser beam at the cougar and push the red button!" Scott was standing completely still now, as the cougar was crouched and ready to spring at any moment.

Anna struggled to steady her shaking hand as she held the stunner out at arm's length. The laser light was trained at the midsection of the cougar.

In a split second, the cougar jumped at Scott. The stunner caught him in mid-air, as Anna pushed the red button with all her strength. She closed her eyes and prayed that it would work.

A whoop of joy brought her eyes open. There on the

ground, lay the cougar motionless.

Everyone sighed in relief and the Murphys unashamedly thanked God for saving them out loud. Scott assured them he had improved the previous stunner model and they could escape before the cougar could move.

Scott called the search and rescue emergency number with his cell phone. Then he retrieved his backpack and replaced the rest of his scattered belongings.

Anna gently examined Kayla's foot, which revealed that the cat's claws had left deep gashes, about three inches long, across the top of her foot. Anna quickly disinfected the wound, and bound it in gauze.

It was decided that they would walk as far as they could. But only ten minutes later, the small procession halted.

Limping and in pain Kayla protested, "I can't walk another step."

Actually Anna was impressed at how far Kayla had already gone; after all, this girl was used to shopping by limo. They were now in an open clearing, which they hoped would be wide enough for the helicopter to land.

Thirty minutes later, a helicopter approached. Using his baseball cap, Christian flagged down the pilot.

The rescue helicopter spotted them and was able to land several minutes later. Two paramedics jumped out and made their way over to assess the extent of Kayla's injury.

Anna had tried to stop the bleeding to Kayla's foot as much as possible.

"There's not enough room for everyone," one paramedic yelled.

Christian waved them off. "Anna and I will walk," he said raising his voice to be heard over the rotor blade of the helicopter.

Kayla's foot was swiftly bandaged and both paramedics helped her to the helicopter.

Anna and Christian stood back against the pine, side-by-side as they watched the helicopter take off. The pilot waved and looked straight at Anna and Christian as if he knew them.

Shock was etched across both their faces. "Quincy?" Anna and Christian asked together in astonishment. "This cannot be possible!" The same pilot who had been flying when Christian had gone skydiving in Florida was now here in Colorado?

Disconcerted, Christian and Anna hurried down the trail as fast as they could go.

Unknown to them a silent figure watched as they hurried away. He wasn't happy about his campsite being discovered by a group of amateurs and he was going to do something about it.

Chapter 24
Answers

Anna walked into the downstairs library, armed with an envelope of the developed pictures she had picked up earlier and a mystery novel. A few minutes later, she was comfortably seated in an overstuffed leather recliner reading. This was the first chance she'd had to relax since they had arrived in Colorado.

Twenty minutes passed when Christian sauntered in, munching on an apple, and plopped himself down on the seat next to her.

Anna looked at him, lowered her book and said, "Mrs. Song Le called to thank me for helping Kayla and to let us know that she's resting at home now. I'm so glad she's doing better—although I doubt we'll ever get her on another hike!"

"You can say that again! Did you ask if that was really Quincy piloting the helicopter?"

"As a matter of fact, she said the pilot recognized us and said to tell us hello!" Anna looked thoughtful, "I guess he has recovered."

"You're probably right. Anyway, I'm really glad Kayla's doing better," Christian said.

"It's a miracle that she only received minor lacerations on her foot," Anna added.

"Hey, can I see those pictures?"

"Sure," Anna said as she reached for the envelope on the end table. "These aren't of the dig. It's the first roll I took of the house when we got here." She handed them over.

Christian idly flipped through them, silently admiring Anna's expertise. For some reason one of the pictures of the house arrested his attention. He studied it with a frown, trying to figure out what was out of place, and then it dawned on him.

"What's wrong with the picture?" Anna asked, and teasingly remarked, "Did I take a really bad shot of you?"

"No, look." Christian brought the picture over squatting down beside her chair.

In the corner of the picture was a camouflage Jeep. Only partially in view, they could still clearly see that it was parked on the side of the Sullivans' house.

"Rick's Jeep?" Anna asked looking at Christian. "I don't remember seeing it when I took the picture."

"That's got to be Rick's Jeep. How many camouflage Jeeps have you seen around here?" Christian agreed. "But the thing I can't figure out is, why?"

"Remember when we first arrived? Mitch announced that a Mr. Richard something was here to see Mr. Sullivan," Anna said thoughtfully.

"Yeah, Anna, you're right! He was about to say his last name when someone cut him off. I remember Mr. Sullivan hurried into his office. Richard–Rick! Same name."

Anna took the pictures back and quickly looked through the other ones of the house. Nothing else revealed the Jeep. The more they looked at the one photo, the more certain they were sure that it was Rick's.

"There has to be a rational explanation," Christian stated. Yet his voice didn't hold conviction.

"Explanation maybe, but rational?" Anna asked. "I mean

there are things that just don't fit together about Grandma's and Grandpa's friends."

"I know exactly what you're talking about, Mr. Sullivan smoking, for one thing. Because of Grandpa's respiratory problems, he never hangs out with anyone who smokes."

"There's the accent change from the shock during the near-accident while we were in the limo," Anna added. "And, the room that had wigs, were they Mrs. Sullivan's? I've never seen her hair any other color but white."

"And, the way the Sullivans are never available to talk to Mom and Dad on the phone," Christian paused for a moment to think. "And the way they're spending an incredible amount of money."

"The question is, why would they be dealing with Rick Lane? I mean, he's not quite in the same league. Why would they want him over?"

"Anna what if we're wrong? There could be good reasons to all of our suspicions. I would hate to be faced with the embarrassment of accusing them . . . "

"Yeah?" Anna said, "Accusing them of what? How about trying to buy our affections through gifts?"

"Anna!" Christian stared at his sister, "accusing them of not being who they seem."

"Okay, so all we need is some evidence to support our hypothesis," Anna finally answered.

"Hypothesis? I definitely don't have an educated guess. The only thing that could prove they are the Sullivans is to get Grandma and Grandpa here and ask them."

Anna wrinkled her nose. "Very funny. Just the same, let's not say anything in case we're wrong. I don't want to have to explain why we thought they were, as you put it, not who they seemed."

"Deal." Jumping up, Christian began to pace back and forth across the room in front of the floor-to-ceiling bookshelves. One thick book's title caught his attention, and he reached to pull it out, "Hey! Look at this book, it's called *Unlocking the Mysteries of Creation*." As Christian pulled out the book, a loud click

181

sounded.

Anna turned to look at Christian. She was just in time to see part of the bookshelves swing inward. Anna gasped, clasping her hand over her mouth.

Both looked in shock as there was an open door leading into a little room.

"What is this place?" Anna asked in awe.

"Looks like a hidden computer room. I wonder why it's here?" Christian asked.

"How'd you get it to open?"

"I tried to take the creation book off the shelf. It must have triggered the door to open." Christian said, as he took a step inside.

"Christian, get out of there," Anna scowled. Hearing a scraping sound, she turned toward the doorway, but when she looked no one was there. Against her better judgment Anna followed Christian to the room's doorway.

"Come and see," said Christian. "This is what Scott meant by a smart house."

Anna stepped into the room, which had two computers on a large wooden desk. Oak shelves and cabinets lined the wall. Papers, files, and books dotted the room, along with a scanner and several printers.

"Look at this, Anna! Surveillance cameras must be picking up these images." The screen was divided into quadrants, with each area flashing a different room in the home. The rooms kept changing. Within a few minutes time, they could see the whereabouts of every employee and their activities!

"No wonder the employees are often looking over their shoulder like someone is watching them. Someone was," Christian flatly stated.

Anna pleaded, "Christian, let's get out of here!" She was too late. The door swung shut! Anna and Christian twisted around, but there was no handle on the inside.

"We're locked in!"

A deep voice with a southern accent spoke through the door. "That's what ya'll get for snoopin' 'round. Now we'll have to deal with you two."

Although the man's voice no longer had a heavy Irish accent, Anna and Christian were both certain it was Mr. Sullivan.

"Mr. Sullivan?" Christian called, "It was an accident we didn't mean to . . . Mr. Sullivan? Mr. Sullivan?" Christian finally gave up and turned to Anna. "I guess we're stuck," he grimly stated.

"What do you mean, stuck? How could he do that?" Anna asked angrily.

"I think it's time to pray," Christian said, grasping his sister's hand. They both bowed their heads while Christian asked for the Lord's help and guidance. As soon as he opened his eyes he noticed another computer!

Christian walked over to the other computer and sat down at the keyboard, "I'll bet I'll be able to find out everything we need to know with this."

That was an understatement; when he moved the mouse, a message flashed up on the screen. "Enter password," it read.

"Oh, great! Now what do we do?" Anna said.

"Guess," Christian said, simply.

"Guess! It could be anything! Numbers or words or both!"

"Okay, let's see. I'll try something easy to start with," Christian said. "The Sullivans are from where?"

"Ireland," Anna said.

"Yep," Christian typed I-R-E-L-A-N-D

Access denied.

He typed in Ireland backward.

Access denied.

"Okay, no sweat, Anna. Think of something else that has to do with Ireland."

"How about St. Patrick?" She questioned.

Christian quickly typed the name and hit "Enter."

Access denied.

He typed it in backwards.

Access denied.

"Rats! Hmm, I've got it! A lot of people think St. Patrick was Irish, right?" Christian suddenly grinned, but Anna shrugged.

"So? I don't understand."

"Where was he originally from?"

"Christian! What is this a history lesson? If you think you know the password, then tell me!" Anna fumed.

Christian spelled E-N-G-L-A-N-D.

Access denied.

Christian typed in the letters D-N-A-L-G-N-E.

Anna held her breath as Christian pressed Enter.

"Yes! We're in!" Christian cheered.

Chapter 25
Pieces Fit the Puzzle

"We are in big trouble!" Christian exclaimed as he read the contents of the computer screen.

"Us or the Sullivans?" Anna asked, trying to keep up with the rapid clicking of the mouse as Christian moved from one screen to another.

"Both," Christian responded.

"Look at this. The Sullivans took money from their own philanthropic organization and deposited it into Rick Lane's account. Something really strange is going on!" Christian said, pulling his eyes away from the computer and reluctant to look at his sister.

"Oh, Christian, how can that be?" Anna asked, although she wasn't particularly fond of the Sullivans. Yet they were, after all, friends of her grandparents.

"You know, something just isn't right about all this. The Sullivans are just not what I picture our grandparents' friends to be. Buying us presents is one thing, but their attitude toward others I just can't put my finger on it. They seem mean spirited."

"Go on. What else?" Christian encouraged Anna, not wanting to say what was on his mind because it was so far fetched.

"The Sullivans are nothing like I expected. I just can't imagine Grandma and Grandpa hanging out with the Sullivans. Can you?"

"Nope! I don't think the Sullivans are who they say they are."

"Well we've already said that but we have no proof."

"Do you remember the day we went shopping with the Song Les?"

"Yeah, so?" Anna said, impatiently, waiting for Christian to explain.

"Well, Scott had watched some TV show about criminals, and they talked about these people who stole other identities—and millions of dollars."

Anna's eyes grew wide. "And you think the Sullivans are the criminals? How could our grandparents be friends with them?" Anna asked. Then, smiling added, "Wait! You mean the Sullivans are not the Sullivans. They are the criminals impersonating the Sullivans! Oh, Christian, you're brilliant."

"Thanks, I try." Christian laughed, then became more somber, "But we're stuck in here with this knowledge. What do we do now?"

"You know I should be mad at you. Why didn't you tell me about the TV show criminals earlier?"

"I didn't make the connection. We've been so busy since we've gotten here. This hasn't been a relaxing vacation. It's been hard work!" Christian grinned, "Now I'm sounding like Dad."

"Hey! I've got a brainstorm!" Anna said, excited. "Does this computer have a modem? Can you get online?"

"Yes, of course. This is state-of-the art, even if there isn't a phone in here."

"I wonder why." Anna added, "but, not to worry, I have a plan. We'll e-mail Scott."

"Great idea! If he's wearing his e-mail pager device he had with him at lunch, the other day, he might instantly get the message. That guy is incredible and always experimenting with

186

his gadgets."

"Yeah, but you like him," Anna smiled.

"You're right!" Christian agreed. "How does this sound? Reference: Danger, danger, danger! Scott, help! We're trapped in the closet behind the library bookshelf on the north wall. Think the I.D. Snatchers are impersonating the Sullivans. Use extreme caution! Get the police ASAP. Thanks, A. and C."

"Sounds great," Anna said. She watched her brother, send the message off with a click of the mouse. A box appeared on the screen saying the mail had been sent. "But, I think this is going to take a major miracle. First he has to have the e-mail device with him, and second he has to respond quickly, so we'd better pray." They held hands, and closing their eyes in prayer, asked the Lord for His support, help, and the wisdom to deal with the situation.

"Amen." They each noted the other's relief.

"Well?" Anna asked, looking at the computer screen.

"Nothing," Christian said. "Do you have a plan B?"

All of a sudden the computer sounded a cheerful tune, like the cord of a harp. Both of them jumped! "We've got mail!" Christian said, the first to recover.

Scott had not only received their SOS, he was currently online! He could speak to them in real time using typed words.

Both laughed as they read his response, "Never fear, Scotty's here!"

"Great to hear from you, man! Can you call the police?" Christian typed out the response and hit the enter key. They both waited until the harp played again, signaling another response.

"Yeah, but I got a better plan."

Christian typed back, "This is no time to be a hero. These people may be the criminals and are possibly dangerous. Remember the TV show?"

"Got it covered. Will get you out. Later, dudes!"

Christian sat back deflated. "I hope he knows what he's doing and doesn't think he needs to save us single-handedly."

"Maybe in the meantime we'd better get as much evidence as we can to prove these people are not the real Sullivans."

187

"Another great idea, Sis!" Christian grinned, opening a desk drawer and looking for a disk, "You're on a roll."

"Yeah, thanks," she playfully punched her brother's shoulder as she began inspecting the cramped quarters.

"Well, it was a good idea, but unfortunately I don't see a blank disk... Wait, this computer is networked. With the password, I can take this information and send it to my computer!"

"Great, I'm glad all those years of pushing buttons have not been wasted," Anna said.

As Christian worked out the details of sending the information to his system, Anna continued to look at the walls. Something was amiss to her photographer's eye. She looked at the painting, hanging beside the door where they had entered. It was a painting by the artist, Cézanne, but the subject matter was strange. Anna was familiar with the painting. Her mother loved art and she had taken a course in art appreciation. It was entitled *Le Chateau Noir*, which was French for The Black House. It was not one of Cézanne's major works, and even if authentic, she couldn't imagine that this painting would be hidden away.

Anne ran her finger around the edge of the painting, not really knowing what she was looking for. A small gasp escaped her lips as her finger caught on a small spring, and the painting popped open on a hinge. "Christian, look!" Anna exclaimed.

"Just a minute; I'm almost done. One more thing and ... there, finished," Christian said, looking up from the screen, "What's the..." his voice trailed off as he swiveled in the chair to face Anna.

The painting had been hiding a safe!

Chapter 26
The Mystery Couple

"How did you find that?" Christian asked in surprise.

"Never mind that! Do you think the combination is in the computer?"

"Well, there is only one way to find out!" Christian turned back and typed a few words to do a system file search, "Yep! Here it is, under a file called passwords. Are you ready?"

"Wait a minute, Christian," Anna hesitated. "I know we are stuck in here, but do you think we should pry any further? Don't you think we have enough information for the police?"

"All we know for sure is some people, supposedly calling themselves the Sullivans, are using money from a trust fund to pay off Rick Lane. Even if we don't like him, as far as we know the only shady thing is some diamonds in his waistpack. We don't have any *proof* the Sullivans aren't who they say they are. Besides, we think the fake Mr. Sullivan shut us in here."

"Okay, give me the numbers," Anna was resigned that this was necessary.

"25-53-72" Christian said.

Anna punched the numbers into the digital display, and a green light beeped three times. "Now what?" Anna asked, expecting the safe to spring open. Several seconds later a red light flashed and a nasty buzzer sounded.

Christian stood looking at the face of the safe. "Maybe you need to pull the lever down, once the numbers are pushed. Hit the clear button and begin again."

Anna punched in the numbers again. This time when the green light and ensuing beeps sounded, she grasped the large lever and pushed down forcefully. The safe door sprang open. "Well, it's not the crown jewels, but there are a lot of papers in here," Anna said.

"Let's see." Christian turned so he and Anna could both look over the papers. There was a mortgage deed and closing documents to the house, insurance papers, and more.

"Great, just a bunch of boring stuff," Anna said.

"Maybe we can compare the signatures on these documents with the Sullivans signature."

"Right, and how do we do that?" Anna asked.

"Not us, the police," Christian said.

"By that time, the imposters will have escaped." Anna frowned.

"I doubt that they are in the living room, enjoying the view, and waiting for us to catch them," Christian said. "If they really wanted to harm us, they wouldn't have locked us in here."

"Maybe it wasn't Mr. Sullivan who locked us in here after all," Anna said.

"Or maybe he did," Christian said, suddenly triumphant. "Jackpot!"

Anna's eyes widened as she watched her brother hold up a slim black case. A piece of paper fluttered to the floor, which Anna reached down to retrieve. The black case opened to reveal a photograph. There a kindly looking, gray haired, smiling elderly couple looked up at them from the photo. Above the photo, apparently taken on a cruise ship, were the words, "To my darling wife on our fiftieth wedding anniversary... all my love,

Johnson."

"Now those two look like people our grandparents would be friends with!" Christian laughed.

"Look at this note." Anna read, "These diamonds are a small token of the everlasting love I will always have for you."

"The diamond necklace we found in Rick's waistpack!" Christian said, "Why those creeps. That means the Sullivan 'wannabees' stole the diamonds and gave them to Rick."

"But why?"

"Maybe Rick is a fence and could sell them?"

"But what was Rick's pack doing in Lawrence's tent?"

"I don't know; maybe they're accomplices?" Anna said, as she carefully placed the note in the picture frame case and put it back into the safe along with the other papers. "Poor Mrs. Sullivan, I'm so glad we found her diamonds."

"And, let's hope it is still in your back pack," Christian said.

"We should have called the police when we got back to the house," Anna lamented.

"Why would we?" Christian asked. "We didn't know they didn't belong to Rick, or that they were even real."

"I guess we should have believed Kayla when she said they were real," Anna said remembering the conversation. "As much as she shops, she should know!"

Just then they heard a noise outside the door.

"Hey! We're in here!" Christian hollered as he pounded against the wall.

"I can hear you, but I don't see you." Scott's muffled voice could be heard through the wall.

Christian quickly told Scott about the secret doorway and how to access it. Within minutes Scott's smiling face was in the doorway, "Greetings prisoners! So glad I could free you," He bowed ceremoniously as the Murphys exited.

"Are we glad to see you!" Christian said. "Did you call the police?"

"Are the Sullivans here?" Anna asked.

"Whoa, one question at a time. Yes and no. Yes, I called

the police, who are in the other room and should be in momentarily to ask you some questions, and no the Sullivans are not
here."

"I can't believe it! They got away! Oh, where are the
police? We've got to stop them!" Christian said in exasperation.

Anna and Christian looked around the library where they
had been, just a short time earlier, discussing the suspicions they
shared about the Sullivans. Now, after finding the hidden room,
their suspicions were confirmed, only to find the Sullivans had
escaped.

"This is awesome!" Scott came out from looking at the
hidden surveillance room. "I've got to build one of these in my
house." He closed the door and sat beside his friends.

Anna and Christian both burst into laughter, and were
glad their friend had helped ease their tension. "I can't just sit
here," Christian said; "can't we use your Song Glider and try to
find them? They probably took the limo."

"Sorry to disappoint you. The Song Glider is being repaired, and the limo is in the garage," Scott said.

"Everyone, let's gather in here." Several plain-clothes
police officers and two in uniform walked in, escorting the entire
staff. "My name is Sergeant Jeffrey P. Wiggers. I want to ask
you all a few questions and then we will talk with you individu-
ally and privately. Please understand no one is to leave until we
are finished. Any questions?"

"Has something happened to the Sullivans?" Hilary asked,
worriedly as she wiped her hands on her apron.

"We believe the Sullivans were impersonators. The *real*
Sullivans are in Ireland. We've been in touch with them. Mrs.
Sullivan's mother has pneumonia. Mr. Sullivan was here last
month for the closing of this home after it was built and he claims
he hasn't set foot on the premises since that time."

The staff had taken seats around the room wherever available. Several began speaking in hushed tones. Anna and Christian looked at the group. She nudged Christian and whispered,
"Hey look, there's Sam and Cindy." Cindy wore her straight
blond hair back in a ponytail and Sam's hair was cut short and

slicked back. Both looked bored by the entire procedure.

Christian shrugged, "So, I guess they're working today."

"Everyone, please if I can have your attention. I know you'd like to get this over with as soon as possible. First, did any of you see the Sullivans, that is, the impersonators leave here today?"

"Yes, I did," Cindy said, in a slightly breathless voice. "Mr. and Mrs. Sullivan left in the Porsche around 10:00 am. They said they were heading to the mountains for the day."

"Yeah, she's right; I got the car ready for them," Sam said, in agreement.

One of the police officers turned and whispered to another and quickly exited the room.

"Have any of you seen anything suspicious?" Sergeant Wiggers asked.

For some reason Anna and Christian did not speak up. They didn't want to reveal what they had found just yet. Scott looked at them in surprise, yet only a raised eyebrow revealed what he was thinking. *Why didn't they mention the hidden room?*

"I've got a doctor's appointment in town, and I don't drive. Can my husband and I be excused?" Cindy asked.

"Yes, after we've taken everyone's statement. We'll begin with you two." One of the officers walked over to the couple with a clipboard.

Scott took the chance to ask the Murphys, "What's up? Why didn't you mention the room?"

Anna looked at Christian and he nodded, "Are you thinking what I'm thinking?"

"There is something strange about those two. Look at Cindy's eyes. Doesn't something look funny?"

Scott tried to look nonchalantly over at Sam and Cindy, without looking suspicious, "Huh, what do you two see that I don't?"

Anna rose, facing the seated boys. "Cindy has one blue and one green eye!" she hissed.

"I take it she doesn't normally?" Scott asked.

"No she normally has green eyes, and Mrs. Sullivan has

blue. The exact color blue of Cindy's one eye. I'm going to find the officer that went out and see if I can tell him our suspicions. If we all walk out, it will look strange we don't want to call attention to ourselves."

"Good idea, Anna," Christian answered. Pretending to be relaxed, he stretched out with his legs in front of him.

Anna walked to the doorway where an officer stood guard and spoke quietly to him. When he heard what she had to say, the officer allowed her to pass. He casually unclipped his gun holster and stood ready. Sergeant Wiggers had finished questioning several of the staff and walked over to the officer. The two spoke in quiet tones.

"Who, what, where?" Scott hissed, "Explain! What suspicions?"

Christian leaned over and whispered, "I think those two are the criminals!"

"No way," Scott said impressed.

"Yes, way," Christian smiled. "It's their eyes. They are the impersonators. I'm almost positive. I wonder who Sam and Cindy really are?"

"Wow, a double impersonation. The TV show didn't say anything about that!" Scott said, impressed.

"See you later," Cindy rose from her seat with Sam in tow, "I hope you catch those crooks."

Christian watched, poised for something to happen. Sergeant Wiggers smiled at the two as he and the officer stood aside and let them pass. Christian bolted upright wanting to do something, but he stood there rooted to the spot watching helplessly. He couldn't believe it! The people that had stolen millions were walking out the door and getting away!

Chapter 27
The Truth Will Set You Free

Once the two had left the room, Christian raced to Sergeant Wiggers with Scott close behind.

"Sergeant, I think those two are the criminals." Christian told him what he suspected.

"Son, I think you're right."

"Well, are you going to let them get away?" Christian demanded.

"Now calm down. We've got it under control."

Anna joined them smiling. "Boy, are they in for a surprise!"

"Will someone please tell me what's going on?" Scott asked.

"Linda and Douglas Bailey alias, Cindy, and Sam Norris and also impersonating Johnson and Sarah Sullivan. They were not only impersonating the hired help, they were impersonating the Sullivans! In this way they could keep tabs on the household and be in touch with the real Sullivans." Sergeant Wiggers said.

"How did they ever manage to pull it off?" Anna asked. "The real Sullivans have a large staff of employees. Apparently one of their managers hired Cindy and Sam to oversee the transition of the Sullivans to this new home. They had glowing recommendations, albeit fraudulent." Sergeant Wiggers said. Cindy and Sam decided to impersonate the real Sullivans, while they were out of the country, and embezzle as much money as they could without raising too much attention. We've known of the I.D. Snatchers for some time but since they are masters of disguise it has been difficult to find them. Thanks goes to Anna for noticing her eyes."

Anna smiled, "It wasn't difficult."

They all walked back into the library, and Sergeant Wiggers told them they had placed a tracking device in the car of the suspected criminals. "We still need some evidence that they are the I.D. Snatchers we have been looking for. I am hoping they will lead us to where they have stored some of the stolen items."

"I can show you the records in the computer, sir." Christian quickly showed the officers the hidden room and the information in the computer. Another officer was dispatched to pick up Rick Lane for questioning. He had a lot of explaining to do, especially as to why a substantial amount of money was deposited in his bank account.

The Murphys told the sergeant about finding the diamonds, in what they believed to be Lawrence Edelman's camp, in the mountains. Anna ran up to her room to retrieve the waistpack with the diamonds from her backpack. She handed them over to the officer. Anna explained about reading the note in the safe and believing the diamonds belonged to the "real" Sullivans.

"We would have called you earlier, but I completely forgot about the diamonds, especially after we had the run-in with the cougar. Besides, we weren't sure the diamonds were real."

"These will be taken into custody. They might be needed for evidence later on," Sergeant Wiggers said.

"The only thing I don't understand is where Lawrence fits into all this," Christian said. "Did he or didn't he have anything to do with Rick?"

"Well, actually, we know all about Lawrence," Sergeant Wiggers told them.

"What!" Christian asked incredulously.

"Yesterday, he turned himself in. And, the only person I can blame is you and you and you." The sergeant pointed a finger at each of the Murphys and Scott.

"What did we have to do with it?" Anna asked in surprise, "we've never even met him."

"Well, we may not have met him, but we found where he lives," Scott reminded them. "I called the police with the coordinates to his hideout."

"Well, son, we haven't had a chance to check that out. It was off the beaten track you know, but we didn't need to. Lawrence saw you sneak into his campsite. He followed you, and came in, after you took his stolen property." The sergeant was enjoying speaking in riddles.

"We knew it didn't belong to Lawrence because I recognized the waistpack as Rick's," Christian sighed.

"We took it because we thought Lawrence stole it from Rick. We planned to return it to Rick," Anna explained."

Scott interrupted, "Okay, I admit it, it was my idea to look inside."

"Lawrence was afraid, that he would be blamed for stealing the diamonds. He and Rick had known each other for several months. Rick was able to track him down and find his hideout. They struck an agreement to work together to save the environment."

"Rick said that?" Anna asked, surprised.

"Well, he didn't mean it. He just wanted to use Lawrence to do his dirty work. You see, since Lawrence was known for his yellow buttercup, Rick decided it would be a good cover for any pranks he wanted to play. When things got a bit rough, like the severed rope that endangered Christian, Lawrence couldn't come out in the open and insist on his innocence. No one would believe him."

"It doesn't make sense. There has to be another reason

Lawrence would want to work with Rick." Christian thought aloud.

"Rick promised him a way to make easy cash working for the Sullivans. Lawrence says he declined the offer."

"But, how did Rick's waistpack get into Lawrence's campsite?" Scott asked.

"Lawrence admitted that he took it. He was angry with Rick for making it look like he was a sinister criminal. It's one thing to take some shovels and pick axes to protect the environment, but quite another to cut climbing ropes and sabotage tires."

Sergeant Wiggers said, "You see, I've known Rick a long time, and he wasn't too happy about not being second-in-command at his brother's big dig. Now that we suspect him of working with these criminals, maybe as a front to sell some valuables, I'm more apt to believe Lawrence's confession is truthful."

"You think he would sabotage his own brother's dig?" Anna asked.

"No, he wasn't trying to harm his brother's dig, Anna. He was trying to get rid of Luke," Christian said. "With Luke out of the way, he would be second in command. Luke was meant to climb first, with the cut rope, not me. And Luke's tires were deflated. Now we know he tried to throw us off his trail by placing the buttercup and pretending these things were done by Lawrence."

"That makes sense, but I guess we'll find out more once we pick him up for questioning," Sergeant Wiggers said.

The officers gathered their papers and left within the hour, promising to check back later if anything was found.

"Wait until our parents hear about this," Anna looked at Christian, eyes glowing; "I think you, as the oldest, should make the call."

Christian looked at his sister and groaned, falling back on the leather sofa in dismay.

Scott looked at the two of them incredulously, "And you think I live on the edge with my daredevil flying machine! You two just helped to solve an awesome mystery!"

"I can't believe Kayla missed all this," Anna cried, "She

198

loves to be in on the action."

"I'd rather call and tell her all about it." Scott said. "Hey, maybe I'll call TV's 101 Most Wanted. They may want to interview you. Then your parents can find out by watching the show. What do you think?"

The Murphys dissolved into laughter. That would be totally unacceptable, but they could dream, couldn't they?

Epilogue

"Oh it's great to be home," Anna beamed at her family. She and Christian were seated on the large leather sofa in the family room. The room had high ceilings, a fireplace, large arched windows, and French doors leading to an open-air deck, which stood open. Andy snuggled between Anna and Christian, as they each held one of the twins. Dr. and Mrs. Murphy sat a short distance away on a matching leather loveseat and smiled at their brood.

"I wasn't so sure you'd want to come home, what with adventure, mystery, excitement, maids, butlers and limousine drivers..." Dr. Murphy laughed, teasingly.

"Yeah, Anna is sorry she had to return the fur coat!" Christian teased.

"Right, I don't think so!" Anna laughed.

"Well, I'm just glad you are home and safe! To think we entrusted you to live with criminals!" Mrs. Murphy's eyes flashed, "I should have been more persistent and realized something was odd when the Sullivans were never available to take my call. You see, I often spoke with Sam, I mean Douglas, or whatever his real name is! He apparently was screening all the calls through his cell phone."

"It's all right Mom," Christian assured her, "Obviously you were praying for us."

"And believe me, every prayer was answered!" Anna emphasized.

They had spent the last hour recapping all the news from their adventure. Rick had been apprehended and had indeed been found guilty of the sabotage at the dig site and for collaborating with the criminals. Dr. Lane admitted to police that his brother had often tried to capitalize on his discoveries and had a network of buyers, just what the criminals needed in this case. Meanwhile, the big news had reached them that the police had apprehended the masters of disguise, Linda and Douglas Bailey, also known as the I.D. Snatchers. The tracking device in their car had led the police to a loaded warehouse with incriminating evidence, which would keep them off the streets for a long time. Most of the money had been returned to the Sullivans' account. Meanwhile the real Sullivans would soon be traveling to Colorado to finally enjoy their vacation home.

"I want to know what you thought of the *T. rex*?" Dr. Murphy asked, "The photos are astounding Anna, so thorough. I think you've moved up to become a world-class photographer!"

"Thanks Dad," Anna beamed at her father's praise. "It was awesome, Dad, and the most exciting thing was when they got the results about the red blood cells."

"Yes, I've spoken to Luke about that. He has invited me to the university lab to study the results."

"Wow, Dad! When are you going?" Christian asked, impressed at the invitation.

"I'm not," Dr. Murphy draped an arm around his wife, "I like my job as it is. I can pick and choose when and where I work. Sometimes I do have a pressing deadline, but for the most part I'm free to spend time with my family."

Just then the doorbell rang, and Mrs. Murphy went to answer it. "Jack, kids, I think you'd better come out here."

Everyone trooped to the front door and looked out. "Hey, cool! Whose Jeep?" Christian asked, pointing to the gleaming new white and beige Jeep that was parked in the driveway.

Mrs. Murphy held up the keys and said, "Apparently yours and Anna's."

"What?" They both exclaimed.

Jack looked at his wife in astonishment. "I hope you didn't buy it."

Mrs. Murphy laughed, "No, but the Sullivans did. It appears that this is their way of thanking our kids for saving the rest of their fortune!"

Anna and Christian looked at each other, eyes gleaming, but cautiously asked, "Are you going to let us keep it?"

"We'll talk about it," Dr. Murphy said, trying to look stern. Everyone walked out to admire the car.

"What's this?" Andy asked, pointing to the box at the door when they went back in.

"It came with the Jeep. The delivery man said it was for Anna and Christian," Mrs. Murphy replied.

Anna and Christian opened the box, and then laughed at the contents. Scott Song Le had sent along some of his favorite gadgets for their future adventures. He was sure they would need them and wanted to be kept posted on how well the gadgets worked. He also included a note stating he was on his way to learning more about Jesus through the study of His creation. The family returned to the living room to look at the assortment of two-way radios, a GPS device, and gas saving fuel additive.

"Dad, you're really not going to go see Pete's dragon?" Christian asked.

Dr. Murphy laughed. "I didn't say I wouldn't go see it! I'm just turning down the job as part of the research team to prove that the red blood cells were truly found. As far as I'm concerned, we already have the proof, which is found in the Scriptures. Besides, for Dr. Lane to insist that his staff disprove it is absurd."

"He really gave us a hard time about our beliefs," Christian said thoughtfully; "I mean, at times he seemed to like us, and at other times he was so defensive. He wasn't open to anything about a Christian world view."

"That's not surprising, you know. Most people become defensive when Christians remain steadfast in their beliefs. Besides, this isn't the first time that unfossilized bones have been found. We must continue to pray for those who cannot see," Dr. Murphy said.

Anna and Christian exchanged looks. They knew that faith is the evidence of things unseen and the truth, as in this case, will set you free.

Dear Readers,

Christina and I have enjoyed bringing you this action-adventure novel interspersed with the truths about creation. Many aspects of this book deal with recorded scientific findings, while the storyline is purely fiction.

All of the characters and the story are fiction. Rocky Mountain National Park does exist in Colorado, as does "the Diamond," which is known as one of the greatest alpine walls. It is found on Long's Peak, the highest mountain in the park. Diamond Peak is ficticious as is the dig site, a fictionalized ledge.

All of the references to the geologic column, the Flood, references to dinosaur-like creatures in Scripture, circular reasoning, and more are true. You can find these and much more exciting information about creation science in any of the references we provide at the end of this book. I am especially delighted to tell you that the reference to the red blood cells being found in the dinosaur bones are, in fact, real. The report can be read on many creation science sites, which I have also listed in the reference section.

You see, in writing this book, all we knew was that Christina wanted to write about dinosaurs and Colorado. The Colorado part was easy, but what dinosaur discovery could we bring you that would be really exciting? Well, a science news article caught my eye. The *T. rex* bones were found in 1990 in Montana. Some sections were not completely fossilized, and yes, red blood cells were found within. The tests I talked about in the book were real. They did test for iron with laser lights and inject red blood cell portions into rats for three weeks. The results showed that the cells were indeed blood cells.

I pray that you have enjoyed reading this novel, even half as much as we have enjoyed writing it. It is a joy to work together with my daughter. If you haven't guessed, she is the one with the wild imagination for many of the action scenes. We will continue this series as long as the Lord inspires us to write. May God bless you as you enjoy the beauty of His Creation. Continue to always search for His truth and proclaim it in love!

About the authors:

18-year old Christina Gerwitz has always been homeschooled and learned her love of writing at an early age. She enjoys being with her family, her friends, reading, playing basketball, watching movies, swimming and has an advanced certification in SCUBA. Her love of the Lord is evident to those who know her. You may e-mail her at Writer4JMJ@aol.com

Felice Gerwitz is owner of Media Angels a publishing company dedicated to producing quality materials for homeschooling parents. She has enjoyed writing this second novel in the *Truth Seekers Mystery Series* with her daughter. She has homeschooled her children since 1986. Neal, her oldest, has graduated; Christina's graduation will coincide with the printing of this novel and she will go on to a university in the fall. Felice will continue to homeschool Nicholas, Anne, and Michael. Her husband Jeff continues to be her best friend and strongest supporter. Most importantly he is a wonderful spiritual influence in her life. You may contact her at by e-mail at MediAngels@aol.com, or on her web site, which contains more titles she has written at www.MediaAngels.com or www.Virtual-Field-Trips.com.

The authors would like to thank the following people for without their help this book wouldn't be possible:

Our family for giving us the time to write and help with running the household.

Frank Sherwin, Jill Whitlock, Catie Frates and Michael Oard for their expertise in the area of creation science.

To John Michael Hogmire for his expertise in rock climbing.

For our cover models: Michael Scanlan and Megan Hogmire and to John Michael who just "happened" to have rapell gear we could use for the shoot. To David Frantz the cover graphic artist. Praise God for his tremendous talent and willingness to work under short deadlines!

Readers and editors, thanks for your wonderful suggestions and insight:

Kathleen Oare, Margaret Ann Gerwitz (grandma), Kristina Krulikas, JoHannah Sherwin, Megan Hogmire, Gabriela Martinez, Kinley, Trish Engvalson and family, George, Geneva Mock and family, Pat Wesolowski and family, Forest and Shirley Dunbar, Beth Blikstad, Beverly Oard, and Rhonda Howard. A very special thanks to Jan Sherwin who unselfishly gave of her time to make this a much better end product and her many useful suggestions for rewriting!

References

Bliss, Richard, Gary E. Parker and Duane T. Gish, 1980. *Fossils: Key to the Present.* Santee, CA: Institute for Creation Research.

Frates, Catie, 1997. *The Creation Interpretation. A Basic Biblical View of Science and Natural History.* Gresham, OR: Noble Publishing Associates.

Gerwitz, Felice and Jill Whitlock, 1997. *Creation Geology: A Study Guide to Fossils, Formations, and The Flood!* Ft. Myers, FL: Media Angels.

Gerwitz, Felice and Jill Whitlock, 1994. *Creation Science: A Study Guide to Creation!* Ft. Myers, FL: Media Angels.

Gish, Duane, T. Ph.D., *Dinosaurs by Design.* Green Forest, AR: Master Books.

Ham, Ken, 2000. *The Great Dinosaur Mystery Solved!* Green Forest, AR: Master Books.

Larson, Neal, *Dinosaurs & Birds The Sue T. rex Story.* Black Hills Institute for Geological Research, Inc. May 2000.

Morris, Henry, M., Ph.D., *The Profusion of Living Fossils,* Acts & Facts. Vol. 28 No. 11 November 2000 Online Issue No. 3.

Morris, Henry, M., Ph.D., *Dragons In Paradise,* Impact No. 241. Vital Articles on Science/Creation, July 1993.

Press Release, 1-21-2000. *Dino-Bird Controversy.* National Geographic, NationalGeographic.com.

Richards, Lawrence, O., 1989. *It Couldn't Just Happen.* Dallas, TX: Word Publishing, Inc.

Tejada, Susan, 10-15-1999. *Dinosaurs are not Extinct: Their Descendants Fill the Sky.* National Geographic. NationalGeographic.com.

Wieland, Carl, *Sensational Dinosaur Blood Report.* Creation Ex nihilo 19(4):42-43 September-November 1997.

Wieland, Carl, *Dinosaur Bones: Just How Old Are They Really?* Creation Ex nihilo 21(1):54-55 December-February 1999.

Resources:

Censored Science: Catie Frates
    CensoredSci@ithink.net

Institute for Creation Research
    www.ICR.org
    PO Box 1606 El Cajon, CA 92022 (619)-448-0900

Answers in Genesis www.answersingenesis.org
    PO Box 6330 Florence, KY 41022 606-727-2222

Genesis Ministries and Creation Adventures Museum
    www.genesisministries.com
    25308 Rampart Boulevard Punta Gorda, FL 33983
    Creation@strato.net or ForestDunbar@yahoo.com

Creation Studies Institute
    5601 N. Federal Highway Ft. Lauderdale, FL 33308

Media Angels
    www.MediaAngels.com
    MediAngels@aol.com